TO CRUSH THE SER

D1578873

Yashar Kemal was born in 1923 in a village on the cotton-growing plain of Chukurova. He received some basic education in village schools, then became an agricultural labourer and factory-worker. His championship of the poor peasants lost him a succession of jobs, but he was eventually able to buy a typewriter and set himself up as a public letter-writer in the small town of Kadirli. After a spell as a journalist, he published a volume of short stories in 1952, and in 1955 his first novel, *Memed, My Hawk,* which won the Varlik Prize for the best novel of the year. It has sold over a quarter of a million copies in Turkey alone and has been translated into every major language.

Yashar Kemal was a member of the Central Committee of the banned Workers' Party. In 1971 he was held in prison for 26 days, then released without being charged.

Kemal, many of whose books have been translated into English by his wife, is Turkey's most influential living writer and, in the words of John Berger, "one of the modern world's great storytellers".

522 002 49 9

Yashar Kemal

TO CRUSH THE SERPENT

Translated from the Turkish by
Thilda Kemal

HARVILL
An Imprint of HarperCollins*Publishers*

First published under the title *Yilani Öldürseler*, Istanbul, 1976
First published in Great Britain in 1991 by Harvill
an imprint of HarperCollins Publishers,
77–85 Fulham Palace Road,
Hammersmith, London W6 8JB

9 8 7 6 5 4 3 2 1

BRITISH LIBRARY CATALOGUING IN PUBLICATION DATA

Yasar Kemal *1922–*
To crush the serpent.
Rn: Kemal Sadik Gökçeli I. Title II. Yilani
öldürseler, *English*
894'.3533 [F]

ISBN 0-00-271111-7

Set in Monotype Garamond 156 by
Butler and Tanner Ltd, Frome and London

The Random House Group Limited supports The Forest Stewardship
Council® (FSC®), the leading international forest-certification organisation.
Our books carrying the FSC label are printed on FSC®-certified paper.
FSC is the only forest-certification scheme supported by the leading
environmental organisations, including Greenpeace. Our
paper procurement policy can be found at
www.randomhouse.co.uk/environment

Printed and bound in Great Britain by Clays Ltd, St Ives plc

TO CRUSH THE SERPENT

H ASSAN must have been six, perhaps seven, the year his father was murdered.

Eagles were circling above the Anavarza crags, wing to wing. A cloud gathering in the distance cast its shadow over the swamp and glided on towards Dumlu Castle. The flowers of the asphodels reached up to the sun, alive with bees, iridescent, black, blue, yellow. Blue cardoons thrust their spikes out among the crags, bright blue.

Hassan was scuttling along the rocks, partridge-like. The dizzy heights below made his head whirl. He had reached the eagles' nests he was after, but had not found a single egg or chick yet. At his approach eagles started up from the wall-like cliff, the flutter of their huge wings shaking the air.

The rocks were warm under the spring sun, with blue milkwort, yellow crocus and purple clover growing in between. The wild thyme was almost in flower, its scent already heavy.

Hassan's last hope was a nest at the foot of the steep incline. It was almost inaccessible and, once, he had slipped and remained hanging out from the rock over a void the height of ten minarets at least. If he hadn't got hold of that wild fig snag, if it had snapped he would surely have been dashed to pieces even before reaching the bottom of the precipice.

To Hassan the many many springtime scents were the

very odour of the Anavarza crags. The bees and lizards and nestlings, the rattlesnakes and arrowsnakes all smelled of the crags, even people did, a pleasant honeyed heady smell. The rain on Anavarza smelled different from rain in other places. It was redolent of wet fragrant rock, and the clouds overhead too emitted a special smell, unforgettable for Hassan, as had been the smell of gunpowder in the darkness of that night. Gunpowder has a different odour among the rocks in the night, not at all as it has on the plain or on earthy soil ... The night had reeked of gunpowder and the sound of shooting had sounded far out in the distance, whizz whizz whizz, echoing, re-echoing.

The crags of Anavarza are these echoes for Hassan, the blast of shots, that smell ... Blood-stained eagles had been circling in the sky above ... He remembered it all. Forever imprinted in his mind was the terrible memory of that crepitating night and those eagles gliding in the early morning sky ...

Hassan was nine years old and lived alone with his mother. But for some time now he had not been able to look her in the face. If he happened to meet her eye he would be shaken to the core. Even before sun-up, when she offered him a pat of butter, fresh from the swinging-churn, he would spread it quickly over the warm bread and, retreating to the furthest clump of trees, would crouch down there to eat. It seemed to him as if he had not seen her for ages.

It was very hot that morning. There was a weight on his heart and he did not know what to do with himself. It was always the same on mornings like these. Sometimes he would rush out madly into the village, not really knowing where he was going, what he was doing.

This valuable rifle, its stock all inlaid with mother-of-pearl, had been given him when he was only seven, and ever since then he'd been firing it at every living thing under the sun, birds, goats, jackals ... Even at people. Hassan had three uncles, his father's brothers. Not one of them ever rebuked him so much as once, whatever he might have done. The village was a small one and people were all more or less related to each other. It was not long since they had settled here, having been nomads before that. His uncles, his father, when they were Hassan's age, had minded the flocks up in the high Binboga Mountains. Their dwelling was a vast seven-pillared black tent. Strange with what pride they still evoked the memory of that tent ...

He finished his bread and butter in the pomegranate garden and went to his rifle. The mother-of-pearl glinted bluely in the first rays of the dawning sun. For a long time he stood gazing at it, rapt, his arms hanging, his head tilted to one side.

His mother was bustling about in the yard, busy with the morning chores. How beautiful she was! And so young ... Like a little girl ... His father had been much older, so old his hair and beard were quite white. Hassan remembered him quite clearly. How long her hair was, reaching down to her waist ... Everyone said she was the most beautiful woman in the Chukurova, perhaps in the whole world. Many a young man in these parts wanted to marry her, but she refused them all, for that would mean being parted from her Hassan, her one and only son. Hassan's uncles were adamant. The boy must stay with them should she choose to leave. If she married she would never see her son again.

The river Jeyhan was running low in a silvery glitter. For days on end Hassan had been hunting for kingfishers on its banks. When he spotted the mouth of one of their long burrows, he hung a thin-meshed net like a bag all about it and waited until the birds darted out and got caught in the net. Then he would put them into cages which he fashioned out of white gourds. How blue they were! There never was such a brilliant blue anywhere in the world. As he gazed Hassan would drift into a blue dream, his whole being suffused in a blue glow.

Then there were the swallows. No one in this village could catch them, no one but Hassan. When he put his mind to it he would capture half a dozen swallows in one day, tie them to a string and fly them all through the day till night came. But he always let them go, always, even though sometimes with the string still attached.

And up in a cave on the Anavarza crags were the eaglets he had been raising secretly for some time.

Every morning at break of day Hassan left the house, only to return when it was quite dark and no one was about in the village. And always, wherever he went, he took his nacre-inlaid rifle with him. And always with him this impulse to run away, never to seen his home again. Many a time he'd walked right on to the next village, but something, perhaps fear, had made him turn back. Once he'd even made friends with a shepherd from Farsak, beyond Kozan. He could very well have stayed with him, but ...

Yet he knew he must not remain in this village. Or else it was his mother who should go. Everyone was against her here. He felt the hate in the air. It was suffocating him. What was the good of staying on, of putting up with all this enmity? None of his relatives on his father's side would speak to her, neither his grandmother, nor his uncles and aunts. His beautiful, beautiful mother ... Bearing it all, only because of him, Hassan ... People said that his uncle Ali, the youngest of his uncles, did not really hate her. He wanted to marry her, but she would not have him.

And so his uneasiness grew day by day. Not a living creature could he turn to, confide in. He was alone, hemmed in on all sides, unable to break out of the iron circle around him. The boys of his age avoided him and he avoided them too. There was only the elusive Salih, but he never spoke a word. All the better. Hassan could pour out his troubles and talk and talk and never be interrupted. Ah, to have such a friend ... How good it would be ...

If Hassan had not been able to forget himself in the blue kingfishers, the swirling eagles of Anavarza, the rattlesnakes, he would surely have died.

First there had been that stealthy sound outside. His father's spoon remained suspended in his hand. He looked at his mother. She bent her head. Hassan was watching them both. The sound outside grew nearer, then stopped altogether. His father's hand moved again. He went on eating.

It was evening. On the meal-cloth before them was a tureen of *tarhana* soup, a roast chicken and a platter of *bulgur* pilaff, glistening with butter. The odour of that pilaff was to haunt him always.

There was a flash in the window. Then another. Hassan heard the burst of shots only afterwards, or so it seemed to him. The room was plunged in smoke, his father, his mother hidden from his view. He heard his father's scream, his mother's voice raised in anguish, then everything went blank.

When he came to, the sound of shots on the Anavarza crags reached his ears, whistling through the night, raising the echoes. A muffled clamour rose from the village. Then he saw the blood. His father was slumped over the meal-cloth, his hair trailing in the platter of *bulgur*, blood flowing from his body as from a fountain.

Of the man who had burst into the house, seized his mother by the hand and drawn her out through the pall of smoke Hassan recalled only a pair of feverish black eyes.

He had not moved from his place and his eyes were still riveted on his father and the running blood, when people began pouring into the house with racking screams. His grandmother was weeping, and it was only then he realized his father was dead. But there was something else too, something he could not take in. It was his mother who was being blamed for all that had happened.

He remained there, huddling in a corner all through that night, while people came and went, weeping, lamenting, and outside, somewhere, the sound of shooting and shouting never abated. And somewhere too, red flames flickering, flaring ... Blazing ...

The east was only just lighting up when they brought the corpse and flung it into the village square. The dead man's eyes were wide open, transfixed in the same wild stare Hassan had glimpsed the night before. Suddenly Hassan recognized him. This was Abbas, who came from the same village as his mother ... He lay there, all covered with blood, green flies darting over him, strange, silent, bitter-green flies, sharp as a razor's edge, a thing Hassan had always been afraid of.

And then his mother was brought into the square. The uncles were raining blows upon her and her face, her white headcloth, her dress were torn and stained with blood. The villagers started hitting her too, everyone, even the children. And spitting on her ... It was too much for Hassan. Blindly, he hurled himself upon them. Afterwards, they told him how he had bit his uncle's hand, his teeth sinking down to the bone, how like one possessed he had struck out at those beating his mother and spat on them too. A kick from his eldest uncle had finally dashed him to the ground. That's what he had been told, and how his mother had shot out, arrow-like, from where she had been crouching and flung herself upon him. "Don't hurt my son," she had cried. Those were the first words she had uttered since she had been caught. She stood up straight and faced them all. "I didn't kill Halil," she said. "I didn't kill your brother." She pointed to the dead man. "Here's the man who killed him, dead in his turn ..." She stepped close to the corpse. "Alas," she murmured, "alas Abbas, I should have known you better ..." Then, without another look about her, she walked away to her house.

It seemed that on this same night fires had broken out in the village, and several houses had been burnt to ashes. The whole place had glowed like daylight, illuminating even the distant ramparts of Anavarza Castle.

Later in the morning the gendarmes arrived. Their captain, rapping his boots together, started giving orders. A doctor came too. There, under the mulberry tree, he donned a white smock. His eyes were cold, glassy. They stripped Abbas's corpse of its clothes and laid in onto a stone trough. The doctor set about slicing and carving it as though cutting up a sheep. Then he stitched it piece by piece again with a sacking needle. Hassan felt like vomiting.

And there again was his mother. The eldest uncle was trying to draw her towards the dismembered body, but she would not go.

"Come and look, bitch!" he was shouting. "See what's become of your lover, your fancy man you put up to murdering my brother ... Come, bitch, come and look ..."

His mother struggling on the ground, floundering in the dust ... And the gendarmes, the captain, everyone watching indifferently. Not a cry came out of her, not a sound. Just that stubborn resistance . . .

They buried his father with dirges and laments. His grandmother had taken to her bed from grief. She summoned her three sons. "Halil's murderer is not that heathen, Abbas," she said. "It is Esmé herself. You must avenge your brother's death. I may not live to see it, but if his blood is unavenged I will never give up my claim on you, not in this world nor in the next. My son's murderer is Esmé."

It was in jail that I got to know Hassan. They brought him in during the night. All the prisoners gathered about to show their sympathy, but Hassan never uttered a word. His jaws were locked. He could not open his mouth, neither to speak nor to swallow the soup they pressed upon him. Suddenly, his head fell forward and, right there, in the middle of everyone, he fell asleep.

We learnt that after his deed Hassan had fled from the village and hidden up on the Anavarza crags. For three days and three nights they had searched for him in vain. It was his dog who betrayed him in the end. Someone had the idea to set it loose. The dog led them up the crags to the ruins and there, in an ancient Roman sarcophagus, was Hassan. He had even managed to move the heavy stone lid so as to be almost immured and had not stirred for three days and three nights. Who knows how long he would have remained there if his dog had not tracked him down.

One of the gendarmes slapped his face. The villagers stared at him with fear. As he was taken away, as they passed through other villages, people poured out to catch a glimpse of him. Men, women, children, all gazed upon him as at a strange unknown creature, awesome, accursed, weird, almost holy.

And that was how the inmates of the prison looked upon him too. The days went by and he still never said a word to anyone, although several of the prisoners attempted to give him help and advice. He was simply not there, an empty shell, his heart and mind in some other, far-off place. Even eating was a new experience.

His eyes were huge, his face elongated, growing longer and longer as time passed. The skin hung loosely about his thin neck. His clothes, too, were much too large for him. His ears were splayed out like two large sails, away from his head, the tips drooping slightly. Never once did he request anything from anybody, nor did he ask a single question. Twice a day, morning and evening, he cooked his soup on a tiny brazier and, crouching down face to the wall away from everyone, he swallowed it, together with a large loaf of bread. Almost every day his uncles, relatives and other people from the village came to visit him. He would listen to them with apparent eagerness, but his head was always bowed and he never replied to anything that was said to him. Once or twice, I, too, tried to make him talk. He just looked at me, then lowered his eyes and drew back.

All sorts of stories began to circulate in the prison about Hassan, a new one every day. The prisoners made a point of relating these stories in his hearing. The boy would listen, still as a stone, his face frozen, expressionless, his eyes veiled. Only his eyelids fluttered rapidly from time to time. And his colour too would suddenly change to a livid yellow.

The more he refused to talk to them, the more the prisoners set at him. Yet there was something about the boy that held them in check, his terrible story, his level-headed bearing, a certain look in his eyes ... Even the most brazen, vicious convict regarded him with a measure of respect, of secret awe. Lütfi, for instance, that disgusting creature, would make the

9

most scurrilous attacks on him, but the boy never changed his stance. Eyes fixed on his aggressor, he kept on staring until the other, put out by that steadfast gaze, broke off, almost sorry he had ever begun. Yet he went at the boy again and again, this Lütfi, this scoundrel, lost to shame, to all human feeling, urged on by some mad instinct to destroy what is good and true and even holy. Treacherous too, toadying up to a man until he'd got him where he wanted, then turning upon him brutally.

I was curious to see what Hassan would do. So I watched him closely. The first two times he held his peace. At the third offensive he lowered his eyes to the ground and stood quite still.

"Worm, murderer! Bloody son-of-a-bitch! Bastard! Everyone here knows you're a bastard. Get that into your pate. And in this world … A bastard … They ought to kill you, son-of-a-bitch. An ugly bastard like you, his hands steeped in blood, shouldn't be allowed to live another day. Wretch! Pig's balls! Skunk! Aaah, if it wasn't for the Government treating you like a man, I'd wring your neck right here. Your eyes would pop out of their sockets and I'd fling your carcass over that wall. A good feast for the dogs! They'd soon make shit out of you. Dog's shit! Dog's stinking shit! Strutting around this jail, giving yourself airs, a paltry murderer. Pooh, God strike you down, you mangy son-of-a-bitch."

On and on he ranted, Lütfi, foaming at the mouth, working himself into a passion, while the inmates of the prison pressed around, all agog. Suddenly, Hassan stamped his foot hard and pivoted on his heels as though trying to escape, but Lütfi intercepted him with a fresh outpouring of the most unheard-of invectives. Hassan now broke into a sweat. He lifted his head, looked at Lütfi and in the same instant his hand went to the pocket of his *shalvar*.* We hardly saw the switchblade snap open as he lashed out at his tormentor. Somehow, with surprising quickness Lütfi avoided the blow and took to his heels. Hassan spurted after him. Round and round the prison yard they went, Lütfi howling for help, pleading abjectly now. Once or twice Hassan got near enough to wield his knife, but only succeeded in rending Lütfi's old patched jacket. At last, Lütfi flung himself into one of the wards and held the door fast. From there he even started cursing again, after all his craven pleas. Hassan stood at the door and waited silently. Then he went and squatted down against the wall in the farthest corner of the yard. His switchblade was still open and he was glaring at it angrily.

Well, that was the last of Lütfi's badgering. He never ventured near Hassan again.

This time, the prison barons tried to pit Lütfi against me. The creature's attitude had always been so obsequious that his attack was all the more unexpected. He approached me one day and I thought he meant to ask something.

"Yes, Lütfi?" I said, offering him a cigarette.

"Only a lousy bastard, only a dog would smoke the cigarettes of the likes of you," he yelled.

For a moment I was struck dumb. The prison barons stood by, watching for me to strike out at Lütfi so they could then fall upon me in a body. Suddenly, Hassan shot into view.

"Stop, brother," he said to me. "Don't you have anything to do with him. I'm sorry I ever looked at the son-of-a-bitch. He's lower than the most miserable cur."

It was the first time Hassan had spoken since his arrival in the prison.

After that we became friends. I cannot now remember how

* Baggy trousers worn by both men and women in rural Turkey.

11

many months we remained in jail together, but throughout Hassan never talked to anyone but me. He had a certain sympathy for Buffalo Hüseyin, that seasoned old jailbird. Hüseyin would read Hassan's fortune in the grounds of his coffee, but always from a good distance and only to me. And then I would relay his findings to Hassan. The boy must have been gratified, but he never gave a sign of it.

Little by little, he told me his story. We would retire into a quiet corner. Hassan would talk, I would listen, he on his guard, watching warily for any sign of derision, for the slightest disparaging look or gesture, I careful not to discourage him in any way, more and more engrossed by his poignant story. He was a talkative creature by nature, but through the years he had taught himself to keep quiet. In fact, he had become a master at it. But when he did open his lips, when he found someone he could trust, it was a torrent bursting the dam.

Fear was an emotion unknown to Hassan. For him death was a kind of garden of Eden. Nobody had dared take his switchblade away. To approach people as brave as Hassan, who have crossed beyond the pale, into the very valley of death, was no easy thing, not even for gendarmes, bandits, murderers, not even for the boldest of men. Only those, like him, for whom life is a thing of the past, who live in death, could attempt to grapple with him on the same tightrope.

Hassan's friendship made the other prisoners keep their hands off me and protected me from their taunts. If anyone levelled the slightest crack at me, he would find Hassan's murderous gaze fixed on him and would slink away, utterly discomfited.

If he had wished it, he could have been one of the strongmen in that prison, even among all those bloody murderers, this frail-bodied lad whose scraggy neck seemed as if it might easily snap in two.

It happened that we were discharged on the same day, Hassan and I, and a month later I went to visit him in his village. Fifteen days I stayed there and not once did Hassan speak to anyone but me, not to his grandmother, nor his uncles, nor any of his other relatives. It was as though he had taken an oath not to speak to anyone of them again.

"If you hadn't happened to cross my path," he would say to me every so often, "I'd have forgotten all that is human."

Our friendship lasted a long time, but in the end we lost touch with each other.

The period of mourning for his father did not last long. Soon his mother was going about her business as though nothing had happened.

His father had owned a lot of land and plenty of farm machinery, two tractors, a harvester, grain drills ... There were carts and horses too, and the fields sown with cotton, sesame, wheat and rice stretched over several acres on the Chukurova plain. After the murder of her husband Esmé lost no time in taking up the reins of the farm. She was no illiterate country woman and had even completed all the classes of the primary school in her village. It was soon clear to everyone that she was wonderfully efficient and could very well fend for herself without help from the uncles or any other of their relatives.

A couple of months after his father's death Hassan was summoned to his grandmother's side.

"Come, my poor luckless child," she said. "Come to me, my orphan, all that is left me of my dear ill-starred son." And she clasped him in her arms, weeping and keening at the same time. She had the warmest, most moving voice Hassan had ever heard.

After a while she handed him a pair of bright patent-leather shoes.

"These are for you," she said, "a present from your Uncle Mustafa. He brought them this morning all the way from Kozan town ..." And she went on to tell him how Mustafa, the second of his three uncles, had adored Hassan's father, how he therefore cherished Hassan all the more since his death. Then, from an embroidered wrapping cloth, she produced a navy-blue suit. This was from his eldest uncle, Ibrahim, who loved him just as much, more than his soul. Wouldn't Hassan like to put on all these new things and let his grandmother see how he looked in them? No sooner said than done. Hassan cast off his *shalvar* and country shirt and proudly donned his new town suit and shoes.

Though elderly, Hassan's grandmother was still very handsome. Tall and slim, she had delicate features with very large, slanting black eyes. Up to his father's death Hassan had not seen so much as a frown on her face. But now she never even smiled. Day and night she wandered about the village like a grieving lament. All this endless weeping and keening, even if it was for the loss of an excellent son, seemed strange to Hassan.

And now, as he stood before her in his new clothes, she suddenly smiled for the first time and her face lit up. Hassan was relieved. That dark sorrowful look did not become her at all, he felt.

He spoke up and told her so.

The grandmother sighed. "Ah my child, my Halil's one and only keepsake," she said, "it's hard, it's agony for a mother to lose her son. It's a pain like no other. I will not go to my grave without seeing my son avenged. And if I do, I shall not rest in peace. My bones will rattle, my eyes remain wide open ... How can I bear to see the one who had my son killed going and coming as she pleases before my very eyes? Walking over my heart, crushing it ... And now planning to leave her innocent little mite in order to marry another man ... Like a bitch wagging her tail to a dog, she inveigled that wretch into killing my son. The earth over his grave still fresh, she wants to marry and make my own darling grandson die of grief. But I said to your uncles, to Ibrahim, to Mustafa, I said to them, let her go off and marry, what matter? My grandson, my Halil's son, so like his father ... Yes, you take after your father and a real man you'll be, just like your father ... Would my Halil's son, my darling little Hassan ever submit to the rule of a stepfather? Would he stay meekly with the woman who's shed his father's blood, who's taken another man into her bed? Would my own grandson ..."

She was holding him close, speaking in sing-song dirge-like tones, the tears streaming down her face.

When she allowed him to leave at last, his head was in a whirl. What was his grandmother getting at? Why was she saying such things? Quite plainly she was accusing his mother, making out that it was she who had killed his father ...

At home he found his mother in a cheerful, bustling mood. She was giving orders to the farmhands, discussing business with the tractor driver and there was nothing about her that could be even remotely connected with what his grandmother had been insinuating. Yet Hassan felt a strange reluctance to face her and when she bent down to kiss him he pushed her away. Playfully, she caught him in her arms, saying how fine he looked in his new clothes, how she loved the bright patent leather shoes, but he froze at her touch and felt his hair stand on end. Esmé straightened up, suddenly aware that something was wrong. She gave him a long long look, then drew a sharp breath.

"Alas," she murmured. "Alas, my Hassan, what have they done to you?" Her face was ashen, white as a corpse's.

That afternoon his uncle Mustafa made an unwonted appearance in their house. He was holding a beautiful rifle, its stock all inlaid with nacre.

"This rifle is for you, Hassan," he said. "It belonged to your grandfather. He bequeathed it to the first man of our family who would have to right a wrong done to us. It's yours now. You can go hunting with it if you like or, when the time comes, take revenge on our enemies. Come, let's go out and let me be the first to see you using your rifle."

They went down to the foot of the Anavarza crags near the banks of Jeyhan River.

Mustafa inserted a bullet into the breach of the rifle. "There," he said, "take it, Hassan. Aim at that white stone. Let's see if you manage to hit it."

Hassan was in seventh heaven. After the beautiful clothes and shoes, this wonderful nacre-inlaid rifle! He had never expected such attention from any of his uncles. They had always looked upon his mother as an enemy and never spoke to her if they could help it. As for his grandmother, she never even uttered her name.

He took the rifle, levelled it and fired. Smoke rose a short distance from the white stone. His uncle handed him another bullet. He tried again. And again. And at last he managed to hit the stone just on the tip.

Mustafa unfastened the cartridge belt from his waist and held it out to Hassan. "Here you are," he said. "From now on, with time, you'll be able to shoot straight. You must practise a lot. Shoot and shoot again and you'll end up being a good hand at it. Marksmanship can only be acquired by steady continuous practice."

Carried away with excitement Hassan was firing without a

break, making the rocks around them smoke. What a beautiful rifle this was! And how loudly the shots echoed back from the Anavarza crags!

"Don't be afraid to run out of bullets," Mustafa told him. "I've arranged with the shopkeeper in Kozan that he should give you as many as you wish. I can get them for you too whenever you ask me. And if you become a good hunter and shoot some francolins, you'll bring me one too. Or stock doves or plovers ... And when you're a really good hunter and bag a hare, I hope you won't forget your uncle!"

The embroidered cartridge belt also delighted Hassan. Finely worked with silk and silver thread were little animal figures, wolves, ducks, birds, tiny rearing horses, deer with branched antlers, gazelles tensed in full flight ... And also a little boy with a laughing face. Just like Hassan ...

They returned home in the evening, Hassan overflowing with joy. He jumped into his mother's arms and kissed her. There was no trace of his strange mood that morning after the visit to his grandmother. All that was quite forgotten. Esmé tried to share his pleasure. It was good that the uncles should begin to take an interest in her son. Yet something painful gripped at her heart. An intimation of she knew not what sorrow ...

Hassan saw the cloud pass over her face. He felt her sadness and ran to kiss her again.

"Mustafa," Esmé said, "won't you stay and have dinner with your nephew?"

Mustafa did not reply. He just shook his head and left the house.

"What did you talk about with your uncle?" Esmé asked Hassan.

"Nothing special," Hassan answered.

"And your grandmother? What did your grandmother say to you this morning?"

"Nothing special," he said again, dropping his eyes.

That night he slept with the rifle and cartridge belt in his bed beside him. And at crack of dawn he dashed out into the Anavarza crags. After that, morning to nightfall, people could hear the crackling of shots from the cliffs and soon all the village knew that it was little Hassan shooting up there.

A fortnight later Hassan came back flourishing a huge hare. Esmé made a nice stew of it with onions and invited the uncles to partake of her son's first game. They all came with their wives and children. All except the grandmother.

Some days later the eldest uncle, Ibrahim, made a present to Hassan of a three-year-old Arab colt. Hassan's happiness knew no bounds. For days on end he could hardly sleep for joy.

The dust raised by passing trucks lingered cloud-like, low over the distant road. Tractors rumbled in the fields. The cotton pickers had retreated into the shade of their wattle huts and were plucking the seeds from the pods. White piles of cotton lay far and wide about the plain. Through the yellowed stubble stalked red-beaked storks, their long necks jerking up and down.

Hassan was walking along the stream. A welter of confused thoughts rushed through his mind as in a misty dream. The clouds cast shadows on the ground before his eyes and moved swiftly on towards the mauve Taurus Mountains. Alongside, the water flowed sluggishly, its surface filmed with dust and chaff.

Hassan's neck was drawn out, longer suddenly. It had taken on a darker hue and was creased like an old man's. He had the air of someone mumbling to himself, or asleep, in the throes of a dream. Broken, incoherent images, familiar voices, saying things ... His grandmother perhaps, his uncles ... Maybe one of the village women, Old Zala, Maid Elif ... People talking, talking, talking, never letting up ... Events unrolling at a giddy pace ... He listened. All the time he listened, more and more enmeshed in this web of talk.

Would Abbas ever renounce Esmé? He escaped from prison and came after her. Esmé pleaded with him. Go Abbas, she said, you're a fugitive now, everything's over between us ... But Abbas would not go. For a while they stood like that, their eyes locked. Someone might see us, Esmé said at last, go Abbas, go hide in the hills. Only then did Abbas go away. He had a brand new Mauser rifle and was bristling with ammunition from top to toe. He waited in the hills. Esmé did not join him. And the next night he was back again, standing in the shadow of the mulberry tree, a tall straight figure, very still. There was a radiant moon that night. Esmé went down the stairs and out to meet Abbas. Her husband, Halil, was fast asleep. Abbas, she said, you must go away. Look, I've got a son, he's seven years old now. Don't do this to me. They'll kill you, these people here, they'll kill me too ... It was no use. Abbas stood rooted there under the mulberry tree, the moonglow about him brighter than ever. He was silent. Abbas go, Esmé urged him, they'll kill you. He never said a word ...

Esmé had heard of Abbas's escape from prison and knew it was a matter of time before he sought her out. His love for her was too strong to overcome. When they had refused to give her to him in marriage, he had wounded three people, maiming them for life. His sentence had been severe and he had been sent to the prison in Diyarbakir province to serve it out. It was then that Halil saw Esmé and fell in love with her. She would not have him, so one night, with the help of six men, he abducted her from her father's house and carried her off to his village. He tried to have her by force, even binding her hands and feet, but Esmé held fast. A week later he achieved his end by drugging her with an opium sherbet. When Esmé came to and realized what had befallen her, she was seized with vertigo and started to vomit. She was bleeding too. Her shame was more than she could bear. Halil fetched a doctor who stopped her bleeding. Then he took her to his house, summoned an imam who married them before God. That very same day the civil ceremony was performed.

For a whole year she never spoke a word, neither to her husband, nor to anyone else in the village. Three times she attempted to run away. Halil found her and brought her back every time. That bitch is no good for you, Halil, his mother said, send the strumpet back to her family before she brings trouble on your head. But Halil only laughed at her fears. Listen to your mother, Halil, she insisted, you can't force a good thing down a person's throat. There's one man already serving time because of her ...

In the end Esmé emerged from her mutism. Everything seemed forgotten. It was impossible to recognize in her the dumb haggard creature of the day, the dead frozen body of the night. The birth of the child had transformed her. She could think of no one else, she saw nothing else in the world but him. She could laugh now, find pleasure in things, even work about the farm. People in the village were beginning to like her. She was always ready to be of help. Whenever a neighbour was sick or in need, Esmé would be the first to be there.

The years passed. The boy was growing up, thriving ...

And now Abbas had come into her life again. Everyone in these parts had heard of him, knew the story of his passion for Esmé. It was a legend on the Anavarza plain. Ballads were still being sung about it, even here, in this very village.

Go Abbas, Esmé said, if you love me, if your love for me is true, go and don't come back any more. He stood there motionless under the mulberry tree, Esmé facing him, silent both of them. Then as day broke, he turned and walked away towards the Anavarza crags. She gazed after him, standing on tiptoe until he was quite lost to sight.

A month passed and he did not come back. Every night Esmé waited up, powerless to resist a yearning to see him again. Then one morning her heart gave a bound. He was there. It was almost light. She hastened down the stairs. Abbas, she said, go up into the crags. I'll come and find you a little later. He obeyed. That morning she slipped out of the house, a bundle of food tied to her waist. Nobody saw her leave the village.

And so it came about that for a month, even more, two months, Esmé held her tryst with Abbas in his hideaway in a cave on the Anavarza crags. Once, Halil followed her, but somehow failed to hit upon the cave. Abbas saw him, levelled his gun and was about to shoot, when Esmé restrained him.

Some time later the gendarmes surrounded the crags and tracked Abbas down. He held out against them for a day and a night, but they got him in the end. As they led him down into the plain to take him to the police-station he managed to give them the slip.

That night he came again to Esmé's house and stood under the mulberry tree, waiting until she came down to him. And there the boy Hassan saw them, clasped in each other's arms.

The next day shots were exchanged up on the Anavarza crags. Two gendarmes were hit. Halil, who had joined in the search for Abbas, was hurt too. The Kurdish Physician tended his wound. He was a long-faced black-eyed man, always cheerful and smiling. Such things will happen, he said, nothing to worry about, nothing . . .

And then that last night . . . Just before the call to evening prayer . . . Halil, Esmé, Hassan sitting down to dinner . . . The flame flaring in the window, the blast of a gun rending the air . . . A scream . . . The smoke . . . And Halil, face down over the meal-cloth, bleeding . . . Bleeding endlessly. And the smell of gunpowder everywhere.

And the dead Abbas being brought down from the Anavarza crags . . .

Afterwards, they cast his body somewhere outside the village to be torn to pieces by wild dogs.

But Esmé would never let this be. Accompanied by one of the farmhands, she set out in the night and snatched his body from the jaws of a pack of ravenous dogs. Then she put him into a sack and, together with the farmhand, they carried him up to the very summit of the Anavarza crags where they dug a grave, making it as deep as they could. And there, at daybreak, Esmé buried Abbas.

The news spread like wildfire. The village was in an uproar. Mustafa, the second of the uncles, had got hold of Esmé and was kicking her. Bitch, he howled, bloody bitch, you put that wretch up to killing my brother, and now you go and hide his body. Where? Where have you put him? I won't let you live. I won't. The body! You'll give me the body or your life . . .

But he could not get a word out of Esmé.

The whole village seemed to be shouting at her, men and women, old and young, hurling abuse, calling her all sorts of names.

For many days the villagers with the uncles at their head

scoured the Anavarza crags in search of Abbas's grave. They found nothing, neither the grave, nor the slightest trace of Abbas.

The stream was creamed with a wrinkled layer of leaves and chaff, dusty, stagnant, dead-still, as though it had stopped flowing.

She seemed to materialize out of the earth beside him, a tall slim figure, with pursed mouth and strong determined chin. Her hair was hennaed and gleamed redly under the black kerchief that she had worn ever since her son was murdered. Leaning on a thick reed staff she came and crouched down beside him.

In the distance Mount Düldül smouldered in a copper glow. The air smelled of sun-drenched burdock. Waves of heat purled down the Anavarza crags towards the stream which meandered on, suspended in the air, a tremulous silvery haze, like an abandoned path.

Not once did Hassan look at her as she spoke, yet he saw the single pointed front tooth, yellowed, the dark face, the silk sash she always tied about her waist, so thin now, ready to snap almost. The red, green and blue fringes of the sash hung down to her knees. Always, ever since anyone could remember, the grandmother had worn such sashes, and even now, draped as she was all in black in mourning for her son, she had not discarded the sash. She would be buried in it too. Certainly she must have willed this.

So much time had passed, yet she was till scouring Anavarza in search of Abbas's body which that bitch of a daughter-in-law had spirited away. She would find it, yes, and throw it to the dogs, make of it food for the birds of prey and, for that, she poured money on the children of the village, living out her days in the unflagging hope that now, today, they would find that body. And ah, if only her other sons had proved to be men, if only they could have dealt with Esmé ...

"Yes my lion, yes my brave little Hassan, there was no man like your father in the whole of the Chukurova. If it had been any other one of your uncles who'd been killed, if your father were alive, my valiant Halil ... Ah, then you'd see ... Not just one woman, but that woman's whole family he'd have wiped out, stock and strain, cutting them up root and branch. If your uncles had been men they'd have seized that woman the very day your father was murdered, dragged her by the hair to my Halil's grave and there, with a sharp razor, they'd have cut her throat and cast her head over here, her body over there ... She would never have been able to flaunt herself before me, that woman, the mother of my own grandson, taking advantage of the fact that she's your mother. If your father had been alive and seen that bitch strutting about like that ... He'd have thrown her carcass to the wild dogs and birds, your father would. Was there anyone like your father? Like the eagles on the Anavarza crags he was. Not like those miserable wretches, not like those uncles of yours ... Aaah, if only you were older, if only your hand could wield a gun ... Then ... That bitch of a mother of yours ... You ... You, yes, only you! You're the son of my Halil, my Halil who was like the eagles on the Binboga Mountains, the hawks on Mount Düldül, the falcons on Mount Aladag. Aaah, my poor Halil ..."

Hassan listened, his unseeing gaze on the creased, scum-lined surface of the water, motionless, not a flicker on his face. A large black and blue butterfly fluttered up and down over the stream. Hassan's eyes followed it, up down, up down. Soon there were more butterflies over the water and then, all in a swarm, they swirled off to settle on a blue-flowering shrub, dyeing it deep blue, a black-traceried mass of blue.

Weeping, she rose and intoned a lament, crying out her son's name, "Halil, my Halil, the noble Bey that you were ... Your son is a good son, yet only a tiny child. And so they live on, those who killed you, basking in your house, eating your bread, usurping your goods, stepping over your grave ... I, a mother, a mother! Your mother ... How can I endure all this? I, a mother ..."

She bent her steps towards the Anavarza crags and sank onto a rock. The sun was setting, but her passionate vibrant lament never paused. A lump rose to Hassan's throat.

"Soon, very soon she will get married, the one who killed you. Another man she'll take into your bed, some vile worthless fellow. And no one, no one to avenge you, only your son, my grandson, and he so young ... Others will take your place in the arms of the one you loved so blindly. Your dear body rotting away in the earth, and she still thriving, prospering over your blood ... Ah my Halil, my brave noble Halil ..."

Her voice rose to a shriek, raising the echoes from the crags, spreading far into the plain below.

"Your orphaned son ... A nacre-inlaid rifle in his hand, a silver dagger at his waist ... Riding an Arab colt ... But alas, the pity of it! Too young yet. Too small to wield the rifle, poor mite, too weak to kill a grown woman ..."

It was dark when he returned home. His mother put some food before him. He could not eat it. She tried to make him talk. He could not say a word. His jaws were locked. Assailed by doubts, she took him in her arms, kissed him, fondled him, talked to him, but she could not make him even look at her.

That night sleep did not come to Hassan.

*

One day he overheard his mother and his Uncle Mustafa talking.

"You may not be to blame, Esmé," Mustafa was saying, "but all the same I advise you not to remain here in this village. Leave your belongings, leave your son. Go, and save your life. My mother won't speak to me any more because I refused to kill you. Ibrahim's ready to kill you any day, and if he hasn't up to now it's because of me, because I wouldn't let him. But I warn you, so long as you're here, alive in this house, my mother will never give up. She wants your blood. Nothing I can do will stop her. The whole village, all of Anavarza plain holds you responsible for Halil's death. So long as you stay ... Even I ... Even I may kill you in the end, Esmé. Go while there's still time. Let no more blood be shed in this house. We can't hold out much longer. If I don't kill you, if Ibrahim doesn't, our sons will do it. My mother will call upon her family, her brothers. She'll find a way. Your death warrant is hanging round your neck. If no one else will do it, she'll persuade Hassan, your own son, to kill you ..."

"Very well," Esmé's voice was calm, composed. "I'll go. I ask for nothing. No money, nothing from Halil's property. Let it all be yours. I'll take my son and go away, back to my father's house."

"No, you can't do that," Mustafa said. "You can't take Hassan away. He must stay with us."

"Then I won't go," Esmé replied. "How can I go without Hassan? I can't be separated from my son."

"Look here, they'll never let you take him away. My heart bleeds for you, sister. I'm telling you, your days are numbered ... Go."

"Not without Hassan," Esmé said stubbornly.

"Do as you like then," Mustafa said. "If you want to die

... Isn't it a pity for you? You're still young. You could ..."
He stopped.

"Never will I leave without Hassan," Esmé said. "Never will I go anywhere without him. How could I? He's all I have in this world."

"Don't you understand what I'm telling you?" Mustafa cried, incensed. "We can't show our face in this village as long as you're alive. You had Halil murdered, you! Everyone knows it. What can be easier than killing you? The meanest dog hereabouts would hold us to scorn if we didn't."

"Don't, my Agha, I beseech you," Esmé said. "If I have to die, it'll be with my son near me. I'd rather die than live without him."

Mustafa rose. He was a tall man, with broad shoulders and a large face. Hassan saw his eyes. They were bloodshot, terrible. The figure of his uncle loomed even larger in the lamplight. Hassan was afraid. Yet he loved him all the same. Mustafa had been trying to help his mother, to save her from those who meant to kill her ...

After this, it seemed to Hassan that an eerie silence fell over the village, over the house. For the first time since his father's death all the talk about his mother had stopped. No one even uttered her name, neither in his grandmother's house nor anywhere else. And as the days passed his mother grew more and more pensive and troubled. All through the night she would sit up, brushing her long hair, or wander through the house, the very figure of fear.

Then one night the front door was kicked open and three men crashed into the bedroom, firing their guns. Esmé was nowhere to be seen. They combed the room with their electric torches and riddled the beds with bullets. One of the men

27

spotted Hassan cowering in a corner, frozen still. He dealt him a vicious kick in the ribs.

"Get up, you wretched whelp, snuggling all this while in that bitch's groin, your father's murderer ..." He kicked him again. "Where is she, the bitch you call your mother? Where's she hiding?"

Hassan was mute.

"We'll find her, never fear, even if she's crept into the serpent's nest, under the bird's wing. We'll find that bitch and kill her, tear her limb from limb. I'll do it with my own hands. I'll never let that whore live on with the blood of my nephew on her hands, my brave Halil, his bones rattling in his grave ..."

There was no sound from Hassan. He guessed who they might be, these men, and where they had come from, his grandmother's relatives who lived up in the hills, her brother, her nephews, all wild cut-throats ...

They ransacked the whole house and, finding no one, left after a parting kick at Hassan. "What kind of a son is that?" they said. "Living cheek by jowl with his own father's murderer ... No better than hogs ..."

Esmé had heard their footsteps in the yard. Slipping quietly out of the room, she had made her escape and run straight to the gendarme station which was situated a good distance away from the village.

In the morning she returned accompanied by a squad of gendarmes. They found not a trace of the men. But Esmé would not drop her complaint. She lodged a deposition with the public prosecutor in which she stated: "My brothers-in-law are plotting to kill me. If I am found murdered, I state here for everyone to know that the criminals are the brothers of my late husband."

Everyone heard about it. "She'll die," the grandmother

vowed. "And I will live to see it. Even if she shuts herself up in an iron chest, she'll die . . ."

Esmé knew it too. Sooner or later they would get her. She lived in constant fear, hardly ever sleeping, sitting up night after night, nervously combing her hair, her ears strained to catch the faintest unusual sound.

In the days that followed, Mustafa came again several times, secretly, in the night, pleading and threatening in turn.

"Go Esmé," he adjured her. "Don't force us to bloody our hands. As long as you're alive, we're dead. How can it be otherwise when before our very eyes you had your lover kill our brother? Get out of this village, Esmé, or we'll have to kill you."

"Kill me then!" she replied defiantly. "I won't go anywhere without my son."

"No one's going to let you take him away. You must go alone."

But Esmé stood her ground. "I'll never do that," was all she would say.

One night Esmé was sitting on her bed combing her hair, when suddenly her hand was arrested and the comb hung in her hair. She turned to Hassan. He was looking at her. Their eyes met and she leapt out of bed. He saw that she had never undressed at all. He rose and put on his clothes, while Esmé went to their chest. As she lifted the lid, he caught a pleasant scent of wild apples. Quickly she took some things out and wrapped them in a bundle. Hassan picked up his rifle and soon they were out of house and village and hurrying along the road.

When day broke they had already gone past Bozkuyu village and were pressing on for Dikenli. Once there, they would be safe at last, for the land around Dikenli was wooded and they could easily lie in hiding if they were being pursued.

But they were still on the bare open country of Bozkuyu, flat as a board, when the horsemen appeared behind them in a cloud of dust. They flung themselves into a hollow and tried to shrink out of sight. In vain. The horsemen unearthed them as surely as if they had put them there. One of them was Mustafa. They seized hold of Hassan and lifted him up onto the back of Mustafa's horse. Hassan made no resistance.

"Farewell to you, Esmé," Mustafa said. "You can go now, wherever you please."

They whipped up their horses and rode off back to the village.

Hassan was so tired he fell asleep the minute they entered his grandmother's house. He had already been slumbering on the horse's back and roused himself just enough to stumble up the stairs where he sank down in a heap at the head of the banisters.

He awoke to his grandmother's mournful voice raised in another of her long bitter laments and pausing only to call down curses on Esmé's head. He heard someone say: "She's back. Came right back to the village when they took the boy away from her." Unhesitatingly, he rushed out and ran back home. Their house bordered his grandmother's yard.

Esmé opened her arms to him, but somehow Hassan shrank back. He could not bring himself to face her. From the big house, his grandmother's laments and curses, raised to an ululating pitch, could still be heard.

After this incident, everything was quiet for a while in the big house and the village. But hardly anyone spoke to Esmé any more. It was as though she did not exist, as though no one called Esmé had ever come to live here.

For Hassan it was worse than before. It seemed to him that wherever he went, whatever he did, his grandmother was there beside him, speaking to him with love, lamenting her son, cursing his mother. As the days went by he began to hear the villagers talking again, young and old, everywhere, whenever they found him within earshot, and always they spoke about his father, of his father's shameless murderer Esmé, of the bereaved, inconsolable grandmother.

The village was asleep. A lone rooster crowed three times and fell silent. Then a dog raised its voice in a long frenzied howl. It was a sound Esmé had always been afraid of, this baying of a hound in the night. Her flesh crept and she muttered a prayer.

Suddenly, Hassan spoke. The room was very dark. He could not even make out his mother's silhouette. If he had, if he'd discerned the smallest movement he would never have plucked up the courage to speak. He knew it.

"Let's go tonight," he said. "Now, this minute. We can take a different road to get wherever it is we want. If they still come searching after us, if they track us down, I'll hide somewhere and wait until they go away, which is what they'll do when they see I'm not with you. Shall we go?"

"All right," Esmé assented.

She had been holding two bundles of clothes and necessaries ready just in case. They set out at once.

The sun had not yet risen when they heard the sound of hooves and saw the five horsemen approaching at a gallop. Hassan flung himself quickly into a dense thicket of brambles and blackthorns.

"You walk on," he breathed to Esmé. "I'll catch up with you as soon as they've left."

She had not gone far before the horsemen overtook her.

"Where's Hassan?" Mustafa demanded angrily. "Answer me or you'll pay for it."

"He's at home, asleep. That's how I left him. In bed . . ."

"You're lying!" Mustafa thundered. "Lying! You were seen, the two of you, running away."

"He was asleep, I tell you. He's not here . . ."

"I'll kill you," Mustafa threatened.

"Kill me then!" Esmé cried. "You've been killing me anyway all this time. Killing me every day! As though it was I who killed your brother! Why don't you take your revenge on Abbas's family? Why don't you go after his brothers? But no! You pick on me, a defenceless woman. You're afraid of them, those Leks, is that it? You'd never dare to take it out on them. Abbas killed your brother and what's more he abducted your brother's wife. Revenge yourself on his relatives then and clear your family's honour."

With a sharp whistle a whip hit her face. Again and again the men lashed out at her. Esmé screamed, but regretted it at once. What if the boy . . .?

Hassan had emerged from the thicket. At his mother's anguished cry, he dashed up and before anyone had time to stop him he was pelting the horesemen with stones. Madly, like one possessed he kept on picking up stones and hurling them with lightning swiftness.

Aah, he was thinking, why didn't I take my rifle? I could have shot them down, I could, every one of them . . .

"And why didn't you take your rifle, Hassan?"

"Because *they* had given it to me. I wanted none of their damned gifts, nothing that had to do with them. I told myself I'd return when I was grown up and get back by force what was mine. I didn't have so many years to wait . . ."

"But why didn't you take a horse, Hassan? You'd have been able to make good your escape then."

"That's what I thought, but my mother wouldn't take anything from that house. I want none of their goods and chattels, she said, not a scrap. Only my son, only my life ..."

Under this hail of stones a couple of horses shied and reared. One of the stones struck his uncle's face. Blood ran down his cheek.

Esmé lay on the ground, her clothes, her hair, her whole person white with dust. He ran to help her to her feet, sobbing uncontrollably all the while.

"Look at him!" one of the men exclaimed. "How can you expect the son of that vicious bitch to be anything but a son-of-a-bitch himself, a wretched pandering whelp! Look how he's clinging to that woman, his father's murderer! Mustafa, what good can you ever look for in such a miserable worm? Why in God's name d'you want him back?"

He spurred his horse at them, almost trampling them down and galloped away. Hassan was hurling invectives after him, when his uncle grabbed him and forcibly hoisted him onto the saddle.

"You can go to hell now, Esmé," Mustafa hissed. "And don't you dare come back or there'll be blood spilt."

Whipping up his horse, he rode off at full speed followed by the other men and only reined in when they had reached the grandmother's house.

The minute he was set down Hassan made a spurt for the road, determined on getting to his mother. They brought him back, struggling like a madman, in a black rage. His face was bleeding, his clothes in shreds, and still he tried to escape from the grip of those strong men as they dragged him into the big hall.

"Truss him up, the rabid dog," his grandmother ordered.

Then she relented. "No, no don't! Don't hurt my grandson."
She drew up to him. "Stop my child, my brave little darling,
stop. You're wearing yourself out. Ah, I know how it is,
there's no one like one's mother. You want your mother, but
look, my brave little one, it's that very mother of yours killed
my son. You can't bring yourself to part from your mother
even though she murdered your father, so how can I, a mother
too, forget that my beloved son has been mowed down in the
prime of life, how can I forgo my vengeance? Isn't that so,
my Hassan, my brave son's son? How can I watch her preening
and prinking about my son's house while he lies rotting in
the black earth? And when she goes away how can I bear it,
how can I live on if she takes with her my son's only keepsake
in this world? Listen my Hassan, if you go, it's the half of my
heart that will go with you ... But I won't stop you. Set him
free," she told the men. "Let my Hassan go wherever he
wants to."

Hassan was still kicking and scuffling, biting the hands that
held him and anything else he could get his teeth into.

"All right, let him go," Mustafa said, his voice suddenly
soft and gentle. "He's a brave loyal lad and won't be parted
from his mother. Very well. For his sake we shall allow her
to come back. From now on not a word of blame will pass
our lips, nor shall we touch a hair of her head. You'll go now,
my friends, taking Hassan with you, since that's how he wants
it, you'll find Esmé wherever she is and bring her back to her
house. What can we do, it's his own father was killed, but if
he's going to turn out a man who can suffer his father's being
murdered without seeking revenge, without so much as a
murmur, then there's nothing for us but to resign ourselves
... It's *his* father who'll never rest in his grave with his blood
unavenged, whose bones will rattle, who'll weep and moan
till kingdom come, who'll shrink in shame when at last in the

presence of Allah and his Prophet . . . Doesn't he know this? Doesn't he know . . ."

They had let go of Hassan. He remained standing in the middle of the big hall, utterly drained, desolate, quite still now. The men were wiping the blood off their hands with dirty handkerchiefs. Hassan's face was bleeding. He did not know it. He felt nothing. His eyes were on his uncle. He seemed to be listening, but his mind was elsewhere. In a trance, he saw his mother making her way back along the road, stumbling, falling, yet pressing on . . .

"Doesn't he know that the curse of his unavenged father will be on him for ever and ever? That Halil will never never rest in peace, that the earth of his grave will never dry? Never never till the end of time . . ."

Mustafa paused. There was an expression of racking grief on his face. The lines of his brow stretched and deepened. He turned this way and that, his hands fluttering, seemed about to say something, then changed his mind, hesitated and fixed a feverish gaze on Hassan. His eyes had grown huge.

"Doesn't he know?" he shouted suddenly. "Doesn't he know that . . .?"

Again he stopped short and fell to pacing up and down the hall, waving his arms distractedly and shaking his fist at some imagined person.

"Doesn't he know that . . .?"

His anguished eyes rested on his mother and the bitter look on his face deepened.

"This is a mother! A mother! How can she bear it when her dear son's bones shake and tremble in his grave . . . A mother . . . Hassan . . . Doesn't he know that . . .?" His voice strangled in a sob.

When he spoke again his tone was weary, yet resolute, as though aware he had no other choice.

"Doesn't Hassan know that the body of the unavenged man will rise from its grave? Every night, ever since he was murdered I have seen my brother wandering about the house, all swathed in his white shroud. Yes, I've seen him and never told a soul up to now. One night, I woke up to the sound of a loud wailing moan, as though the very stones were crying out. I rose and went out, and there was this figure shrouded in white. I realized that the moaning sound came from him and as I drew nearer I recognized him. It was my dead brother Halil, his face all pale, white as his shroud. Brother, I cried, oh my brother Halil ... Slowly, he began to glide away towards the graveyard. I followed him and all in a moan I heard him speak. Tell my son Hassan, he said, tell him not to let my blood go unavenged. Even though my murderer be a woman, even though it be his mother ... And I saw the ground yawn open. Halil sank into his grave, the earth closed over him and the moaning sound was heard no more."

He bent closer to Hassan. The boy felt his breath hot on his face.

"I shouldn't have said all this ..." Mustafa murmured. "A mere child ... Shame on me for having told the boy that his father had turned into a ghost, that he would haunt the world as long as his murder was not avenged ... How could I have done this? How could one expect a chit of a child to take his father's revenge, how, and when the murderer is his own mother ..."

He walked to the door, then turned and said: "Go with Hassan now, put him on a horse too and ride off to find his mother. And when you find her, bring her back home. On horseback, mind you. Since she's our dear nephew's mother, since he wants her, we mustn't let her get tired walking. Though she be our brother's murderer ... Though ..."

He did not finish his words, but disappeared through the door.

As soon as he had left, his wife, Döné, hurried up to Hassan.

"Oh my poor poor child," she mourned, "what have they done to you? You're all covered in blood! Come my poor orphan, come and let me wash your face and hands and then you can go and meet your mother."

She led him out of the room, cleaned him up and stanched and dressed his cuts.

The men were waiting at the gate, astride their horses. One of them reached out a long arm and lifted Hassan up behind him.

As day was drawing to a close they came upon Esmé. She was sitting hunched up on a grey slope by the roadside, oblivious to everything. Hassan jumped down quickly and ran up to her.

"Mother," he cried, "look, I've come to you. We're going back together." Then in a whisper in her ear: "My father's risen from his grave," he said. "Uncle Mustafa has seen him. So have other people too, I'm sure, all swathed in his white shroud and moaning all the time."

His voice was so low it seemed no more than the buzzing of a fly in Esmé's distracted ears. She hardly grasped what he was saying.

Hassan was afraid. This ghost, had he risen from the grave in order to kill his mother?

"What shall we do about him, mother?" he asked huddling up to her. "They say he comes every night and stands at our door. It must be true. I heard him moan one night myself, very faint ..." He straightened up and took his mother by the hand. "Come, let's go."

The horsemen had been waiting by, staring at mother and son. One of them dismounted and helped Esmé onto his

37

horse. Then he lifted Hassan up behind her. They set off, the men walking ahead and leading their horses by the rein.

The whole village was gathered about their house when they arrived. At the sight of Esmé a rumble rose from the silent crowd.

An old man raised his voice. "Esmé, Esmé," he cried. "It's all up with you, Esmé. Halil's risen from the grave. His ghost has been seen by everyone in this village. He wants his blood. His blood! And if he's not satisfied he'll take his son and nobody will ever see him again. Never!"

Without a glance about her, Esmé cleaved through the crowd and entered the house.

An unusual calm fell over the village after that, as though people had forgotten all about Hassan and Esmé and the ghost. How long this lasted Hassan could not remember. Perhaps six months, perhaps a year ... But Esmé was frightened. This sudden quiet after what she had gone through, after the threats made on her life, boded no good.

Then one morning the whole affair flared up again, but not as Esmé had expected.

Kerim, that artful old runaway from the army, was all over the village with tales that went from ear to mouth at lightning speed.

"I've seen him," he announced, straining his long neck like a stork's, "Halil himself, as I was going down the crags above Alikesik last night, a huge figure in a white shroud, glittering in the darkness, his eyes breathing fire. He barred my way, tall as a poplar he was, and bent his eyes on me from his towering height. Stop, O Kerim, he hailed me, do you know me? I do, I do, I said. I know you by your voice, aren't you Halil, Cholakoglu Halil, who's been dead and buried these many months? ... His very self, O Kerim, risen from the grave, doomed to haunt the earth because of my heartless mother, of my degenerate brothers, of my milksop son who's old enough to know better, because of that woman, my wife, my murderer. I have no mother, Kerim, go tell her that. No mother, and no brothers either. I do not know them. My son Hassan, a strapping lad now, ah, but of what use to me when I cannot rest in my grave, when the demons of hell prod me day and night with their burning forks ... He was weeping now, the ghost of Halil ... Ah Kerim, he went on, how can you know the torments I have to endure? You see me now before you, tall as a minaret in this white shroud, but don't you believe it. Those demons of hell never let me rest, never. Every day they change my outward form and shape, every day I find myself transformed into some repulsive creature, now a dog roaming wild in the crags, howling all night long, feeding on carrion, now an eagle flying down to perch over my very own door and from there watching that faithless son of mine, and him carrying a rifle too, shooting birds, rabbits, foxes. Instead of killing all those poor dumb animals why doesn't he kill that wicked one and save his father from this ghostly state, from having to be a snake or a centipede or a cat? Being a cat's not so bad, but ... Once, those demons had turned me into a cat, and what will a cat do, I went straight home, to my house. That woman I took to wife, she looked into my eyes and said, this cat looks like Halil. And thereupon she dealt me such a kick ... And when I wouldn't go she knocked me on the head with a club. She would have killed me, that murderess, if I hadn't fled in time. I still can't hold my head up, such a blow it was. Hear me well, Kerim, go to that woman, tell her that it's she who must save me, since my mother, my brothers, my son have turned out so chicken-hearted, since no one has dared to kill her, not any of my relatives, not my friends, then it's up to her. She must kill herself to save me from being a ghost. After all, it was she who bore me that good-for-nothing cowardly son, she's the one who has sinned and brought all this upon me. Let her then clear my honour, my son's honour, or we shall always be accursed. I shall haunt the world like this, a ghost for ever, and my son will never be able to hold his head up among men ... Tell him, tell my son, my mother, everyone, that it's all up with my soul, that these demons are killing me every minute, now a frog, now a snake, now a snail ... How many times have I not begged for mercy, O demons, let me breathe, I said to them, but that only made them roar with laughter. This is nothing, Agha, we've been kind to you up to now. Why, we can turn you into a hundred thousand tiny button-sized snails and scatter you about the earth so that all the demons of hell won't be able to put you together again in time for Judgment Day and you'll have to appear before Allah in the form of just those hundred thousand snails we'll have turned you into. You'll be the ghost of a hundred thousand snails in the next world ... Ah, it's hard, hard for a man when his blood lies unavenged! God forbid anyone should suffer what I'm suffering! As I listened, trembling of all my limbs, the long shrouded creature who was Halil suddenly disappeared. I looked about me and saw a cat rubbing itself against my legs. I realized this was Halil, but the next thing I knew the cat was not there any longer. Instead, an owl was sitting on the rock opposite me, hooting mournfully. Just as quickly the owl melted away. I heard a hissing sound and there, creeping towards me was a rattlesnake! I fled for my life, stumbling and falling down the rocks, so that I was full of cuts and gashes and had to go to the health man to have them dressed. And he said to me, for heaven's sake Kerim, take care! Halil has put his trust in you, you must do what he wants. You must alert his mother, his wife, his son, all the village. You must tell them the dreadful state he's in. Poor Halil, he mustn't be left to wander about the earth in the shape of slimy snails till doomsday. You, too, will be cursed for ever if you don't tell everyone what you've seen and heard . . ."

For days the villagers could talk of nothing else. Some there were who scoffed at the whole story and made merry with the idea of Halil's being seen as a snail, an owl, a cuckoo or even flying over the village in his white shroud. But others swallowed it all trustfully and began to devise the most extravagant plans to release Halil from his ordeal.

And Hassan was the prime target. People felt that in the long run everything rested with him and that they were duty-bound to bring him to book, to make him see how wrong, how very wrong he was. A mother's a mother, all right, but it was because of her that his own father had turned into a ghost. What son, even the most graceless, could stand by and allow his father to haunt the world prodded by demons' red-hot pitchforks and condemn him to creep about in the shape of a snail till kingdom come?

As for Kerim, he made it his task to exhort Esmé. A hundred times he recounted to her his vision of Halil and his torments, begging her tearfully to heed his message. Esmé was silent. He could not get a word out of her.

In the end he lost patience.

"On your own head be it, Esmé," he flung at her wrathfully. "I've been trying to spare you, but let me tell you this. It's your blood or your son's. That's what the ghost said. I must be avenged, he said, or I'll take the boy away from Esmé. So there! Don't kill yourself and see what'll happen!"

Esmé maintained her stone-like silence.

Kerim gave up and decided to tackle Hassan instead. But somehow he could not get hold of the boy. Hassan knew exactly why Kerim was looking for him, what he would tell him word for word, so the minute he spied him from afar he vanished as if the earth had swallowed him up.

But Kerim had made it his only business in life to get this thing off his chest. Finally, he cornered the boy as he was swimming in a secluded bend of the river Savrun. Hassan was naked and could not escape this time. Resigned, he sat down and listened while Kerim at great length related the whole story of his encounter with the ghost up beyond Alikesik.

"Well, I've paid off my debt to the ghost," he concluded. "You know what the ghost said, you know what your mother did. It's up to you now, Hassan."

At that moment he caught sight of a lizard poised on the pebbles along the bank.

"Look, look!" he cried excitedly. "That lizard there, look! It's your father. See its eyes? So like Halil's black eyes . . . See how it's waving its head as though pleading with us. Look, look! It's been listening to us, wanting to hear if I've told you everything and what you have to say . . ."

A smile flitted across Hassan's face. At this Kerim flew into a towering rage. He rose and stalked off cursing up hill and down dale at Hassan, Esmé, at ghosts and all and sundry.

Words poured over Hassan like rain. The villagers, young and old, had made it their sacred duty, wherever they could corner him, to speak to him about the plight of his father. There was no escape for Hassan. Like a sleepwalker he drifted through the village, caught in a roil of wagging tongues.

Only his encounter with old Dursun shook him out of his daze.

Dursun must surely have been a hundred years old. He could hardly walk any more. His neck was so deeply furrowed that bits of straw and chaff stuck in the folds of skin. His eyebrows hung in thick tufts, hiding a pair of grey-flecked blue eyes. Hassan had never spoken to him in his life and was all the more surprised when the old man waylaid him one day as he was passing by his house.

"Stop Hassan," Dursun said in his thin wheezy voice. "Stop and let old Dursun have a few words with you."

And hooking his cane about the boy's ankle he drew him down beside him and peered into his face with an expression of childlike wonder.

"But how you've grown, Hassan!" he exclaimed. "Why, you're a full-fledged lad now! And these stupid people are trying to stuff you full of nonsense ... Listen to me, my child, your mother's a beautiful woman. I've lived all these years and never come across such beauty as hers. And when a person is so beautiful, and what's more, sweet and kind as an angel, people can't bear it and won't rest until they've killed off this beautiful thing. That's what they want Hassan, your mother's death."

He lifted the long tufts of his eyebrows with his two hands as was his habit and fixed a clear blue gaze on Hassan, then bowed his head and sank into thought. After a while he looked up again and laid his hand on Hassan's shoulder.

"Listen to me, my child, don't let them make you kill your mother. How could anyone destroy this beautiful thing that Allah must have taken a thousand years to fashion, with who knows how much love and care? Such creatures are Allah's beloved ones on earth. Don't you go paying heed to any ghost or to that mangy Kerim and tell your mother not to let herself be upset and kill herself because of those gabbling fools. Esmé is Allah's beloved. If she's killed, Allah will put a curse on us all, he'll rain stones upon us, strike us with pestilences ..."

He stopped and smiled, his kind toothless smile.

"D'you know what I'd do now, right away, Hassan, if I was young?"

Hassan did not answer.

The old man repeated his question again so eagerly that Hassan smiled too.

"What would you do then, Uncle Dursun?" he said.

"Well, well! So you can talk, can't you?" Dursun's smile widened.

"Of course I can!" Hassan retorted. "Provided I find the right person."

"Well then, what I'd do is this. I'd move myself bag and baggage to your house. And if I was thrown out I'd ask for work as a farm hand. And if that was refused, I'd fall sick on your doorstep, anything to be allowed to remain and be able to look at your mother all day long, day after day. And, doing this, I'd go straight to Paradise, for I'll have you know, Hassan that no man who has looked to his heart's content on so much beauty will be allowed to go to Hell. Yes, it's Paradise in this world and the next for the man who has been granted such a privilege. Even now, Hassan, even now, if you take me to your house, if I can look at Esmé with these failing old eyes of mine, with all the fervour left in me ... It's a sin to look at such beauty with eyes that can only see so dimly, but ..."

He fell silent and the tufted eyebrows hid his gaze.

Hassan was delighted. "Oh, do come, Uncle Dursun!" he cried. "Let me take you home and mother will make you some coffee and cook for you too if you wish."

"All right, let's go," Dursun said, trying to push himself up with his hands. Hassan helped him to his feet and they slowly wended their way through the village. People stared. They could put no meaning to this sudden companionship and openly cursed the old man and the boy.

Esmé greeted Dursun with pleasure. It was noon, so she

44

laid out lunch under the *chardak**. A weeping willow to the west cast its shadow over the well and the *chardak* too. Esmé invited Dursun to break bread with them.

The meal lasted a long time. Dursun kept holding up his tufted brows to gaze at Esmé, muttering prayers of thanksgiving under his breath and forgetting to eat. When he did put a morsel into his mouth, it was with difficulty that he chewed it with his toothless gums, reverting again to his prayers. "Thanks be to Allah, praised be Him for granting me this day ..."

He sat with them till sunset.

That night Hassan's sleep was troubled by confused dreams. It was his father always whom he saw, trapped in the swamp by the reed-bed, struggling to free himself, changing into a serpent before his eyes, twisting and turning and sinking ever more deeply into the mire, vanishing altogether, only to reappear as a lizard, a frog, a wide-eyed owl starting up from the swamp with muddy straggled feathers and flapping off into a blackberry bush ... Suddenly the ghost again, wrapped in his white shroud, all wet and slimy now, with gaping bulging eyes that were the owl's really, all eyes, nothing but the owl's eyes, growing larger and larger ... Bearing down upon him ...

Hassan was awake long before daybreak. He rose and stopped a moment to look at his mother. She was fast asleep, her long hair spreading over the pillow. It was dressed in the forty-plait style, intertwined with silver and gold thread and coral

* A summer shelter built on stilts.

45

beads. How beautiful she was, even more beautiful than old Dursun could say ... He stood entranced for a while, unable to tear himself away.

The night before he had packed some food into an embroidered saddle-bag, taking care that his mother should notice nothing. He had plenty of money too, which he stuffed into a pouch hung from his neck. Soundlessly, he put on his best clothes, picked up his rifle and went down the stairs.

The stable was still quite dark and he had to grope to find his colt and saddle it. He rode out of the yard, paused a moment at the gate, looking up at the window of the room where he had left his mother asleep, then guided the horse eastward in the direction of Kozan town. Once out of the village, he shifted into a gallop and only reined in on reaching the town. It was midday by that time. He hitched the horse to a tree and went into a restaurant, the saddle-bag with all his food hanging from his shoulder. He sat down and took some *yufka*-bread out of it, as the restaurant keeper came up to him.

"I'll have the dish of the day," Hassan ordered. He'd been in restaurants before.

"Right away, Agha," the restaurant keeper said. He was a Kurd with long tapering mustaches. Hassan had heard of him.

"We've got a nice sweet too today," the man ventured.

Hassan smiled. "I'll have that too," he said, and added: "I know who you are, Uncle."

"Where d'you know me from?" the Kurd asked.

"Aren't you Sülo the Kurd?"

"That I am! And who are you?"

"I'm Halil's son. You know, the one who was killed by Abbas ..."

"Why of course!" the Kurd exclaimed. "I know you now, you're Hassan, aren't you? How's your mother? I've heard

46

say your uncles want to kill her, but that you won't let them. Well, Hassan my child, your father was a good man, what can I say … I never thought his son was a grown lad already … They say your mother had your father murdered, but don't you believe it. A beautiful woman will always have the gossips after her. Your mother comes from an honourable family. A woman like her would never stoop to have her husband murdered. As for your father, he was a dear friend of mine. We used to go drinking and gambling together. Many's the time we engaged a whole night-club in Adana with all the staff just for the two of us … An eagle of a man he was, your father. In all the Chukurova no one would have dared touch a hair of his head. Only a bloodthirsty reckless man like Abbas … Listen my young friend, don't let them make you kill your mother. I know that's what your uncles are planning. They'd kill her themselves if they could, would have done it long ago, what's it to them to kill a woman, only they're afraid of your mother's brothers. They're very powerful and rich, you know, and would stop at nothing if anything happened to their sister. So you see, your uncles know that if they killed your mother her brothers would descend upon them from the hills and not one of them would they leave alive. Why, they'd wipe out the whole family root and branch! But if you do it, if you were to kill your mother, her brothers would never kill you."

Hassan had finished eating while the Kurd spoke. He looked up at this.

"Are you sure they wouldn't kill me too?" he asked surprised.

"Never," the Kurd assured him. "Only," he added quickly, "don't for God's sake kill her. You'd be damned for all eternity, prodded with red-hot pitchforks by the demons of hell. Whatever they do, whatever they tell you, don't let them persuade you to kill your mother. You won't now, will you, child?"

Hassan took courage. "Where do they live, my mother's brothers, do you know? Perhaps if I could find them . . ."

"I don't know," the Kurd replied. "Your father had told me about them, but I can't remember. When your father fell in love with your mother and carried her away, her brothers were bent on having his skin. If it wasn't for the intervention of all those Chukurova Beys they would have finished him off there and then. Now, look here child, don't kill your mother. You never know, her brothers might kill even you . . ."

Hassan produced a fifty-lira note from his embroidered silk pouch and the Kurd hurried to the safe to get the change.

"Thank you," Hassan said as he rose to go. "Keep well, Uncle."

The Kurd saw him to the door. "Don't let them make you kill your mother," he repeated after him in a low voice. "Anyone who'd kill such a beautiful thing would be damned forever."

Hassan jumped onto his horse and sat for a moment, unable to make up his mind where to go now. The restaurant keeper was watching him intently. Annoyed, Hassan spurred the horse and was out of the town at a flying gallop. He stopped at the ford to the stream. Which way should he go now? Where? If only he had thought to find out where those other uncles of his lived . . . He didn't even know their names. And what if it were all lies? What if his mother had no brothers at all and the Kurd had just invented them to frighten him? But then, when his mother had tried to escape, where had she meant to go to? No, no, they must exist, these brothers. She must have a father, a family, friends, but where? Surely somewhere up there in the hills . . .

Slightly dizzy, he turned the horse's head towards the mountains and whipped it on.

There was a path leading through a wooded ascent. He took it and pressed on between the tall scented blue pines. A smoke haze hung lazily beyond the slope and when he came to the top he discerned the tip of a minaret down in the valley. There was a village there, the houses hidden under the thick curtain of smoke. A cock crowed, dogs barked and the tinkle of cattle bells sounded, slow and tired, as bells will at evenfall.

As the village houses came into view Hassan reined in, struck by a sudden doubt. His grandmother's face rose before his eyes ... Then he heard voices echoing back from the high crags above, a child wailing, an old man calling from one hill to the other ... He could not explain why he felt suddenly so happy, so confident. After all he did not even know what village this was. But his horse had brought him here. It would also lead him to a house. He would leave it to the horse to choose. I'm a guest of Allah, he'd say, travelling to find my uncles ... How would he be welcomed? Why, with pleasure of course, anyone would be pleased to receive Allah's guest. Maybe the inhabitants of this village were Kurds, Alevi Kurds whom everyone said were fine honest people. Or perhaps impoverished remnants of the great Farsak nomads ... Anyway, mountain people were the most hospitable on earth.

The horse ambled on and came to a stop before the gate of a large house with a mud-daubed roof and walls decorated with many-hued earth. An ancient plane-tree spread its wide branches over the front yard. Hassan did not move. His hands holding the reins lay idle over the pommel of his saddle. The horse's tail switched rapidly to and fro, chasing away the flies.

After a while an old man emerged from the house. Screwing up his eyes he took a few steps towards Hassan and exclaimed: "Why, here's a wayfarer to bring us good cheer! Welcome to

49

our house, wayfarer. Hey lads!" he called into the house. "Quick, come here, we've got a guest."

A couple of men ran out and helped Hassan dismount. Then the old man led him into the house. Producing a key from his waist he unlocked a carved oaken door and ushered him into a room furnished with divans all around and spread with real madder-dyed *kilims*, rich in colour and design. The walls were wainscoted with carved walnut from floor to ceiling, and on one of them hung a colour picture of Atatürk standing, his right foot planted forward, a whip in his hand, beside him the head of his chestnut horse, and a blue lake in the background. In this picture Atatürk's eyes seemed unnaturally blue.

The room had begun to fill up with men in homespun woollen *shalvars*. They all bid a solemn welcome to Hassan and took a seat on the divans, their legs folded beneath them. Coffee was brought in and Hassan was the first to be served. He drank his coffee in silence, holding the cup delicately by the handle as he saw the others do.

Then his host introduced himself. "My name is Murtaza," he said. "Murtaza Demirdeli. And what's yours, good guest?"

"I'm called Hassan," the boy replied, slightly embarrassed. "My family are the Cholaks from down on Anavarza plain."

"I know them," Murtaza Agha said.

"I'm Halil's son ..."

"I remember Halil," Murtaza Agha said. "A good worthy man he was, your father. One doesn't often see the likes of him in this world."

"Indeed not," the others concurred. "We all knew him very well. Many's the time Halil Agha lent us his aid down there in the plain. A generous hospitable friend he was in that inhospitable Chukurova."

Of the rest of that evening Hassan only retained a vague

recollection. He was very tired, ready to drop off, and to keep awake he began to talk. It was the first time people had treated him like a grown-up person and he did not want to act as an inexperienced child. So he talked, but what he said he could not for the life of him recall. He must have spoken of his father and told of how he rose from his grave as a snake, a huge rattlesnake, for he remembered the eyes of the villagers wide open, fixed on him in astonishment. Food was brought in too, all fragrant of fresh butter, all, the potato stew, the *bulgur* pilaff, even the bread and yogurt . . .

He fell asleep before the meal was over.

When he woke it was not quite day. He was lying in a bed of white sheets smelling of soap and green apples, and through the open window the scent of wild roses came to his nostrils. He sprang up and ran outside. Beyond the wide plane-tree was a frothing mountain spring. He washed his face and relieved himself behind a rock.

Inside, the bedding had been removed. A large tray stood in the centre of the room. On it was a copper tureen of piping hot *tarhana* soup, smelling of mint, and also butter, honey and village skin cheese.

It seemed to Hassan that people were eyeing him strangely this morning. He sat down shyly, not daring to look at anyone. Murtaza Agha poured some soup into an engraved copper bowl and set it before him.

"Did you sleep well last night, my guest?" he inquired. "Were you comfortable?"

"Yes, oh yes," Hassan stammered, his face flaming. "Very well."

"I'm glad of that," Murtaza Agha said. "I want you to feel at home here. As in your own house . . ."

Hassan cast him a grateful look.

*

He could not say how long he had remained in that mountain village.

A serpent was chasing him all the time, asleep, awake, a huge rattlesnake was on his track. He could not shake it off. It crossed his path on the mountain, among the crags, crept up to the top of the pinetrees after him, followed him into the very room he slept, made him scream out in anguish in the night.

The idea of going to his uncles, his mother's brothers, was rapidly fading away. How could he find them when he didn't even know their names? Something, somehow, kept him from asking his host, who may have known about them.

And suddenly a harrowing thought struck him. What if anything had happened to his mother while he'd been away? What if they had killed her or done even worse to her? He rushed up to his favourite haunt, a spring that bubbled forth high up in the crags, with mauve watermint growing all around it, its fragrance mingling with that of the pines, and stumbled to the ground, assailed by a thousand doubts. How could he have left his mother alone, defenceless, among those monsters, in the jaws of death? Here he'd been, all this time, taking his ease, with not a thought for the hell she must be going through. Perhaps they had already killed her, perhaps . . .

He rose abruptly and stared into the distance. Eagles swooped up and down over the high distant crags and all at once Hassan felt himself shrinking, dwindling to a tiny tiny size, nothing but a black crawling insect. And he knew . . . He knew what he had done. It was all crystal-clear to him now. He had run away on purpose. On purpose so that his uncles should kill his mother . . .

"I don't want to see it. My eyes mustn't see it . . . But she has to be killed, she has to die . . . We can't live on like this, despised by all in the Chukurova plain, my father doomed to burn in Hell forever, to haunt the earth in the shape of a rattlesnake ... She must die. My mother must die ... Esmé must die. She shall die."

That had been the awful thing inside of him all these days, the wicked sinful wish that his mother might die! How could any human being wish for such a thing ...? But what if his mother had indeed killed his father? What if he was not avenged and left to suffer all the torments of Hell? Why should his grandmother feel hatred towards Esmé, for what reason except the one intent, to save her son from rising from his grave every night till kingdom come? Wouldn't Esmé have done the same for him, Hassan? Why then, could Hassan not do it for the sake of his own father?

His head seething, he slumped down there, beside the spring, and burst into tears. Had they killed her? Was she dead already? A feeling of relief was swept away by the searing pain in his heart. He thought of his uncles, obsessed with vengeance, pitiless ... Even his Uncle Ali who had disappeared no one knew where ... Perhaps Ali had done it. He saw his mother's dead body. He saw the soundless green flies, the blood congealed in the dust, the limbs asprawl, the bloated face, the yellow fluid oozing from her eyes ...

He ran back all the way to Murtaza Agha's house. Without a word to anyone, without so much as a goodbye, he flung himself onto his horse and galloped off down into the plain.

How and when he reached the village, he did not know. But his mother's stricken face when she saw him, her anguished scream, he never forgot. She told him later that he had been wounded, his clothes bloodied, caked with mud. The horse too was hurt, a broken leg ... But he must not worry, she'd get him another colt.

*

For days he was laid up, burning with fever. But even when he recovered he would not take a step out of doors, much less venture into the village. He never so much as thrust his head through the doorway. And nobody came to visit him either, nobody asked how he did, not even his grandmother and his uncles. So it was a mystery how that rumour flying about the village came to his ears.

It was his father who had carried Hassan off from his home in the night, swung him onto the saddle of his horse and taken him up into the mountains. There he'd squeezed his hands round Hassan's throat until the boy's eyes popped out of their sockets. Hassan, he'd said, almost strangling him, you miserable wretch, who is it that's left his father's blood unavenged, forced him to haunt the world till doomsday, to burn in Hell forever? What kind of a son are you, what kind of a man? How can you live on like that, without honour, like a beast, and feeding on the hand that murdered your father, too? You ought to be dead with shame, Hassan, you ought to die ...

Weeks went by and still the talk did not abate, until at last one day Hassan dashed out of the house and burst in upon his grandmother.

"I ran away, I, I! No one carried me off. Of my own accord I fled from this cursed place. All because of you ... I never saw my father. I never saw anything ... It's all lies. Lies, lies! You're lying every one of you. Lying!"

He ran out into the village, screaming at the top of his voice: "Lies, lies, lies!"

The villagers stared as they would at a creature possessed and when he barred old Sefer's path, still howling his heart out, the old man started breathing prayers over him to exorcize the evil spirits.

"Poor boy, poor boy," he muttered, "his father's ghost has cast a spell over him ..."

At this, Hassan covered his face with his hands and slunk back home. Throwing himself onto the divan, he remained there motionless, dead to the world. Nothing his mother said or did could draw a word out of him.

But the next day something forced him out into the village again. And it was the same on the following days. Nothing he heard, nothing the villagers said could make him stop at home any longer.

And how tongues wagged!

"A man whose blood lies unavenged will always cast a spell on his son, even if it be an only son."

"A man who's become a ghost will do anything to be relieved from that state."

"God forbid that a man should turn into a ghost!"

"Horrible!"

"And to be an unavenged man's ghost is worse than all."

"Why think! If Esmé should happen to die a natural death now, Halil would have to walk the earth as a wretched ghost forever, in Hell in this world and in Hell in the other!"

"With Allah's will, she won't die a natural death. It would be too awful for poor Halil."

"Better Allah should have given Halil a black stone than a son like that ..."

"But it's no easy thing to kill a mother. A mother's love is too precious to give up."

"And Hassan's only a child yet. Why, if he'd been older, grown up now, he wouldn't have let Esmé live another day!"

"Even so, it's not everyone can kill a mother."

"A man has to be really brave for that."

"Like that very strong man, Zaloglu Rüstem."

"Or the outlaw Köroglu."

"Like Mustafa Kemal Atatürk ... Like the bandit Gizik Duran."

"Or like Karayilan, the Black Serpent, who delivered Gaziantep from the French."

"Ah, how can you expect a poor chit of a child to kill his mother when even a grown man can hardly do it?"

"Now for heaven's sake, what kind of silly talk is that? Trying to provoke the poor boy into killing his mother!"

"No fear! He's got a head on his shoulders, that boy, he won't let himself be gulled."

"Good for the boy! He won't kill her. He won't leave her either."

"What a boy! He's protecting her. Firm as steel he's turned out to be."

"Halil a ghost! What a tall tale!"

"And even if it's true ..."

"Look here, if it's true, then there's many a man in this village will never rest in his grave, with the life they've led, the people they've killed. We'll have a whole crowd of ghosts about the village at this rate."

"All that talk about Halil's not being avenged ..."

"When he has been, well and good. Didn't they kill Abbas just for that?"

"Ah, they're bent on having Esmé killed ..."

"And by her own son too!"

"How long can he stick it out, how long?"

"After all, he's only a child."

"They'll make him do it, mark my words. By hook or by crook they'll find a way."

"Hassan will kill his mother ..."

Hassan was living in a trance. A morbid impulse drove him into the village every day to listen to what was being said about himself, about his mother, his father. And on days when nobody broached the subject he felt cheated, empty, troubled to distraction. He had got so used to hearing people speak about himself that he could not do without it any longer. A sure instinct led him to wherever the talk was going on and he listened silently, tirelessly to the thousand and one stories in which his father figured as a pitiful tormented ghost, his mother as a perfidious whore. And when he heard nothing, he would weave a tale himself, and end up believing it too. He could no longer make out what was real, what was not. His beautiful mother, the ghost of his father seemed to have been transferred into a dream world. And the villagers too, inventing fresh stories, had worked themselves into such a state that they finally believed what a moment ago they knew they had made up.

As for Esmé, it was all over with her. She had no heart to fight any more. Sometimes, even she believed the strange rumours that went around. If she had had the chance to take her son and go now, if they had allowed her to, she would not have done so. A magic circle had been woven all around them, Hassan, Esmé, the grandmother, the whole village.

One morning the villagers awoke to the spectacle of masses of swallows thronging wing to wing in the windows and doorways.

Here in the Chukurova, swallows were familiar household features. They built their nests in barns and stables and were in and out of people's houses all the time. Each year, returning from their winter migration, they repaired their old nests or made new ones, grey knobby mud packs, and set about the business of breeding and raising their young. To destroy a swallow's nest was considered a great sin. The saying went that even if the swallow should nest in a man's eye he must not disturb it. There were a couple of persons in the village who had lost an arm and others who had been struck by the palsy and still went about trembling in all their limbs, all because they had harmed the swallows.

And now, here were all these nests dashed to the ground and dozens of chicks squirming, crushed, dead ... Tiny delicate feathers fluttering everywhere ... Yellow beaks opened wide in terror ...

A furious frenzied hand was reaching at the nests, prizing them off beams and roofs and hurling them down. In stable after stable, barn after barn the same crazy hand ...

The villagers were aghast. Everyone knew whose hand it was, yet they dared not say a word. The village was aswarm with screeching swallows. They swooped down over the chicks, dead or floundering in the dust, and rose again, helpless, uttering heart-rending cries, obstinately circling a couple of yards above them, refusing to be chased away.

People hastened to replace the nests as best they could, but it was obvious that half the chicks had perished, and only a few days later the nests were again found lying all over the place, while frantic swallows dashed through the air and clustered above their dying young.

Again the nests were restored and the swallows diligently set about repairing them. In vain. One night the frenzied hand was at work again ...

Since all the chicks were dead, the villagers saw no point in putting the nests back. As for the swallows, for days they hung about the houses, flitting in and out of doors and windows, then abandoning all hope they disappeared without a trace. Not a single swallow was seen any more after that.

This was a sign of ill omen and an atmosphere of gloom settled over the village.

The ruins of Anavarza Castle were also a favourite abode

for swallows. For centuries they must have built their nests there, under the covered arches and crumbling walls. People could hardly believe it when a shepherd boy, all flushed with excitement, brought the news that the crags around the castle were littered with swallow's nests and that the chicks were being devoured by snakes.

"I've seen them," the shepherd boy swore. "May my eyes drop out if I'm lying. All the snakes of Anavarza, each with a swallow chick in its jaws ..."

Next it was the eagles that the death-dealing hand turned to. Broken eggs and dead eaglets were scattered all over the Anavarza crags, while furious eagles thronged above, whirling in ever greater numbers with a loud swish of wings. A constant burst of gunfire kept them at bay.

It was a fire he was seeing, burning in a circle wide as ten threshing-floors. And into this circle of fire dead eagles kept falling, dead swallows ... Dead yet screeching ... And the rocks were on fire too. Birds, beasts, snakes, the very ruins fled from the blaze, screaming with terror. The bushes, the trees, the houses burst into flames.

And the fire drew nearer and nearer and became a rag. The hand reached out, soaked it with petrol and threw it burning through the door of the grandmother's house. Another burning rag was cast through the window. First the divan caught fire, next the door, then the wooden pillars. A strong northeaster whipped up the flames and the whole house was ablaze in an instant. The fire leapt to the barns and the stables and it was not long before it had passed on to Esmé's house.

Esmé had dressed quickly, and when she saw that the fire was threatening their house, she went to rouse Hassan. But try as she might she could not make him wake up. So she lifted him up, bedding and all, and carried him outside, setting him down under a tree in the yard.

Hassan was watching the flaring flames from under his half-closed lids. He saw his mother dragging their huge chest all by herself down the stairs and out into the yard, but made no move to go to her help.

"Wake up, Hassan, do!" she cried. "You must keep guard over this chest. Everything we own is in it."

The night had turned bright as day. Men in white drawers and shirts, some half-naked, scurried about the yard with pails of water, trying to put out the fire. But the blusterous northeaster fanned the flames even higher, casting fiery fragments far out into the village. A few huts had already been reduced to cinders. Parts of the big house had come crashing down, while from the burning barns and stables rose the bellowing of cattle and neighing of horses.

Hassan continued to feign sleep, while his mother rushed in and out of their burning home to save as many of their things as she could. Every now and again she bent over him and stroked his head.

"Sleep, my Hassan, sleep," she murmured. "Nobody suspects a thing. You did well. It serves them right, those heathens. Good for you."

In the end Hassan sat up and slapped a hand over her mouth.

"Shh!" he hissed. "D'you want to give me away? You'll have me killed. Shh!"

Quickly, he lay back as though overcome by sleep again.

As day was breaking he rose and washed his face at the pump. Weary men and women were coming and going among the devastated homesteads. His grandmother was crouching hunched up against the wall of her yard and his mother was still carrying half-burnt objects from the ruins of their house.

Then he looked up and saw his nacre-inlaid rifle hanging from a bough. A wave of joy swept over him. He had forgotten it inside the burning house, but not his mother, not his lion of a mother!

The burnt-out buildings were smoking gently in the morning haze, exuding an odour of burnt wool and flesh that stuck in Hassan's throat.

With the help of some farmhands Esmé began to move what had been saved from the fire into a small house with a zinc-sheeted roof under the huge weeping willow beyond the wall of the yard. As for the grandmother, she settled into a two-storied frame-walled house right next to it. So they were neighbours again ...

There was much argument in the village as to who or what had started the fire. Everyone had a theory and suspected someone else.

For some reason or other, the three sons of Kizir, a poor peasant, were denounced and arrested, and the lamentations and curses of their mother and wives rent the skies for several days.

Next, suspicion fell upon Black Osman. He was found lying, senseless, in a ditch. Somebody had dealt him four knife wounds.

The rubble from the fire was soon cleared, with all the villagers lending a hand, and master-builders were brought down from the mountain hamlets to start rebuilding the houses.

Hassan never went into the village at all. From morning to night he was out hunting in the reed-bed below Anavarza or sitting and dreaming among the thyme-scented crags.

"Your father, Hassan, your father! I've seen your father! A yellow mongrel dog had been at my heels for some time. It was a moonlit night, bright as day. The dog, his tongue hanging, stopped every now and then and raised its head to bay at the moon. As I turned into Alikesik pass, my flesh began to creep. The mongrel dog howled again and before my very eyes it changed into a tall figure in a white shroud! Then, it was a yellow dog again baying at the moon, and again the ghost. And the next thing I knew, both had vanished, but instead I saw in front of me a huge red serpent, so red the darkness glowed all around it. The rocks, the roads, the growing grain in the fields, the reed-beds, all was bathed in its reflection and a fiery torrent of blood cataracted down the Anavarza crags, sweeping everything before it. The earth shook and Halil appeared again swathed in his white shroud, his face a ghastly yellow. He grasped my hands and spoke. "Listen to me, Mollah Hüseyin, oh brother, hear me well! A terrible fate is mine. Hell would be a blessing in comparison. Three days ago I was an ass toiling for a poor indigent peasant. Before that a wild boar in those mountains ... A month ago I was a dog at the door of my enemy Abbas's mother. A swarm of locusts I was once, and they set fire to me. I hopped off as a single grasshopper and got away ...."

Hassan hid his face.

One day he saw his Uncle Ali standing under the weeping willow tree, signalling to him. He ran up and greeted him with surprise.

"Where have you been all this time, Uncle Ali?" he asked. "I've missed you."

"I was running away," Ali said. "Trying to escape ... There's nothing else I can do, nephew. To the end of my life I'll be a fugitive."

"From whom?" Hassan asked.

"Fate," Ali said. "My fate, and perhaps yours too."

Hassan bowed his head.

"Come, Hassan," his uncle said. "Let's go up into the crags."

"Just let me get my rifle," Hassan said.

They set off for Anavarza Castle. Climbing up the old Roman steps, they reached the foot of the castle walls and sat down on a rock. Trucks, cars, buses, carts and harvesters rumbled faintly on the road below. A long dust-devil was speeding across the plain.

Ali was a tall man, in the prime of youth, but his face was already deeply lined and the skin of his neck creased like an old man's. His hawk nose lent him a hard, severe look. Yet now he seemed stricken by some unbearable sorrow.

"It's too much for me," he burst out suddenly. "I have to tell someone. Hassan, you can help me, only you ... Look, take this. It's an old Bulgarian revolver, an officer's revolver. See how beautifully the stock is worked with nacre and ivory? It was your father's revolver. Your father ... Hassan, he's been pursuing me ever since the night he was murdered. Yes, that very night he materialized before me, a tall shadowy figure, tall as a poplar, pale and white, the nose, the mouth, all its features the very likeness of my brother, yet only an immaterial shadow ... He bent over me. Ali, my dear brother Ali, he said, listen to what I have to say. You're the youngest, the bravest of my three brothers. I depend upon you. My son's still a tiny child, it's you who must avenge me, you who must kill her, she who had me murdered. Don't leave me to wander about the world, a poor ghost ... But I could not kill her. She's too beautiful, Esmé. How could I ever destroy what Allah has so lovingly created? The night your father was buried I took this very revolver you see here and penetrated into your house to kill her. She looked straight into my eyes,

63

a thing of beauty, and spoke. Kill me, she said, kill me but don't let my son ever know an uncle of his did it. You'd make an enemy of him for life, make him hate his father's family. I know you won't rest till you've killed me, so do it now and let me be delivered. She lowered her lovely head. Come on, shoot, she said ... My hand trembled. I could not press the trigger. How could I kill this heavenly woman, the like of which Allah could only make once in a thousand years? Sister, I said, I cannot kill you. I cannot raise my hand against so beautiful a creature of Allah. I'm going away. I shan't stay here. Let someone else kill you if it has to be done. I can't ... And so I fled. But there was no escape from Halil. He was after me in his white shroud, imploring, weeping like a child. I can't do it, Halil, I can't, I kept repeating. If it had been anyone but Esmé, my own mother even, I'd have done it, to save you from being a ghost. But not Esmé, never, never, never! Even you couldn't have killed her, Halil. No man can ... Halil flung himself down of all his length, moaning so dreadfully that the earth shook and trembled at the sound. Kill her, kill her, he wailed, no man can do it, but you must. You must, to save me. You love her, I know it, no man can help falling in love with Esmé. Didn't I do so? And an incurable passion it was ... Yet see me now! See what a horrible fate is mine ... Oh, how he pleaded with me!"

Ali fled to Mersin by the sea. It was no use. Halil was there beside him, looking him humbly in the eye ...

Kill her, kill her, Ali. My grave is infested with snakes and vermin, scorpions, worms, all slowly slowly eating me up, so slowly they'll only have finished on the Day of Doom. Save me Ali, kill her. My son's so small yet, only a baby. And his mother's so lovely ... Ah Ali, I'm still in love with her, yes, even though she had me killed ...

Ali took to flight again. He went to Istanbul. Halil followed him there too. Everywhere he went, Halil appeared to him, forever adjuring him to kill, kill, kill.

"Three times I came back swearing a solemn oath to kill Esmé, to save my brother. But my hand would not obey me. I'll never be able to do it, never. So I'm giving you this revolver, Hassan, your father's revolver. You're a grown lad now, a man. Your father's blood is on your own head from now on."

He rose abruptly.

"But so beautiful a creature ..." he murmured. "No one, no one will ever have the heart to kill her."

He turned from Hassan and without a word of farewell, disappeared down the crags.

He heard old Dursun speaking to him. "Don't heed the devil, son. Don't do anything to your beautiful mother ..."

And the wide plain turned into a sea before his eyes. He'd seen the sea once, down below Payas Castle. His mother had been with him. He remembered all those ships too ...

He was getting into a ship with his mother. The ship sailed through a dense forest and then, before them, barring the way, were the crags of Mount Hemité, but her pointed prow cleaved through and white foam spurted from the mauve crags.

"Stop!" his Uncle Ali shouted. "I'm going to kill you both, now I've caught you together ..."

The ship crashed on through the crags, in a surging foam of mauve. Something like blue rain fell over them and mauve crags spilled down on the ship. Ali had levelled Halil's nacre-inlaid revolver at them. He was going to shoot. Hassan cowered on the deck, sick with fear.

"Stones will rain over the Chukurova plain! Still alive, all of poor Halil's brothers, all, his son too, and none to avenge him . . .?"

He is running through the mauve reed-bed, Halil, his two hands clutching his wound. The reeds are strange, hewed to a sharp point, piercing Halil's legs, his arms, his chest. Save me, save me, he screams, his eyes starting from their sockets, and stumbles into the swamp. Blood gushes from the swamp and Halil's head bobs in and out, in and out of the blood-stained water.

"Snakes will rain on the Chukurova, locusts, vermin, reptiles, huge monstrous lizards . . . Adana, Jeyhan, Misis, Tarsus, all the towns will be destroyed by floods, nothing but swamp will the whole plain be. Mosquitoes and ants will finish off the people . . ."

He saw his father, as plain as can be, holding his sides and laughing at him, contempt on his face. He heard him clearly. "This, a man? This, my son? No better than a beast . . ."

The grandmother had taken to her bed. She looked utterly wasted. There were green circles under her eyes and her hands, too, were tinged with green.

"I'm dying, Hassan," she said. "But I won't let myself die! If I die there'll be no one left to seek revenge for my son. Not one of you has been man enough to do it. And as for Ali, that shameless uncle of yours, he wants to marry that woman, your mother, his own brother's murderer! He's left home and village and is roving up hill and down dale, mad with love for her. Oh, I know she's beautiful, I know her beauty casts a spell on whoever attempts to kill her . : . I've spent a fortune, my Hassan, a fortune trying to have her done away with . . ."

Not even young boys had the heart to kill Esmé . . .

Up in the mountain hamlet of Jankizak lived the notorious Haji Eshkiya,* a retired bandit, who had seven sons, all of them under age, ranging from eight to eighteen years. These children found themselves holding a gun before they were out of leading-strings and grew up in the company of bushy-mustached former bandits, so that in a very few years they could hit a flying crane in the eye, a running rabbit in its hind leg. That was what Haji Eshkiya was waiting for. Minors could not be brought to book . . .

A very rich man he was, this Haji Eshkiya. Anybody with an enemy he wanted to get rid of posted straight to Haji Eshkiya and put the matter to him. Give me one of your sons, Haji, he'd beg, and let him put paid to that enemy of mine. How much do you want? . . . A hundred thousand liras, Haji Eshkiya would say, not a jot less. Think of the risks. Why, they've started throwing children too into prison these days! It's not as though a man's life can be reckoned in money. Not by all the gold in the world it can't. But what can we do, we've had to take up this cursed trade and must make the best of it . . .

The grandmother agreed to pay the price, but the next thing she knew, Haji Eshkiya's son, only a boy yet, had brought back the gun she had given him, without firing a shot. I can't do it, grandmother, he said, my eyes were dazzled when I saw Esmé, I was tied hand and foot. Anyone else, Hassan if you like, I'll kill for you, but not Esmé.

So many many children are reared in the mountains up there just to kill for money, so many a man would do it too just for a price, but not one was to be found to kill Esmé.

"And you can't do it either, my Hassan. You'd never have

---

* *Haji*: a person who has made the pilgrimage to Mecca.
Eshkiya: bandit

the heart to kill your beautiful mother. But mark my words, she'll bring another man into my son's bed, some vermin like that Abbas ... Ah, my son, my Halil, so handsome I hardly dared to kiss him, they have stained him all in blood ... How can I bear it, how can I live on with my son's murderer preening herself insolently in front on me, free to go and come as she pleases?"

A raging northeaster was blowing, uprooting trees, sweeping away stacks of grain, churning up the dust of the roads, shaking the very crags. Eagles hovered in the sky, breasting the blusterous wind.

Hassan was trapped in a circle of fire, and the circle was growing smaller and smaller. Tall flames, the height of five men atop each other, were closing down on him. He felt himself stifling.

"You've not had a bite of food these last three days, my darling."

Beads of sweat stood out on Hassan's brow.

"Darling, if you go on without food like this ..."

Hassan turned on his side. He would not look at Esmé.

"Hassan, if a person doesn't eat anything for three whole days ..."

His face was burning.

"D'you want to die?"

Yes, Hassan wanted to die. Aaah, if only he could die!

No one looked at him any more. People turned away when they saw him, even his uncles now, even the village dogs seemed to shrink from him.

They knew, everyone knew, who had started the fire. Anything could be expected of someone who let his father go unavenged, condemned to be a poor wretched ghost. Such a one would set fire to houses and to people too if he got the chance.

And the swallow nests? Who had destroyed them, killing all those poor chicks? Only a degenerate son like Hassan would harm poor dumb creatures and, God knows, little children too ...

"But look at him! Just look at his nerve!"

"Gadding about all over the place as though he's done something to be proud of!"

"A snake, that's what he looks like, a poisonous snake."

"Holding his nose in the air, damn him, as though ..."

"As though he'd killed his father's murderer."

The burs of the prickly pears he had been picking had stuck into his hands. But no matter. A little fine sand rubbed over them would soon make them come out.

He hardly felt their prick. He was wandering about the village again, anxiously listening for what people might be saying, but nobody seemed to be talking about his father any more, at least not in front of him. After all these months, after all these years of making it their one topic, could it be that they had forgotten the murder, the ghost, everything? No, no, Hassan was sure it couldn't be so. It was just that people fell silent when they saw him, which made him all the more avid to know.

And when one day he managed to ferret something out of another boy, he felt strangely elated ...

Halil was still madly in love with Esmé. Every night, he rose from his grave just to catch a glimpse of her. He longed to make love to her, poor ghost, but that was impossible, so he would probably end up by strangling her, and her bloated body, livid, purple, would be discovered one day among the Anavarza crags.

Swallows, eagles, snakes were pursuing him, all burning in a great fire. Sleep would not come to him at night, and with the first cockcrow he rose and climbed up to the top of the Anavarza crags. There, below the old ramparts of the castle, he stared down into the precipice that dropped into the plain, a sheer descent of rock.

Then, in the half-light of dawn, he began to step along the jagged rocks, balanced on the very edge of the precipice. The plain below was paved with marble, the remains of some ancient Roman edifice. One false step and he would be smashed to smithereens on that marble. He knew it, oh how well he knew it, but still he went on, his heart in his mouth, yet willing himself to walk on, and when he came to the end of the narrow knife-edged rocks, he looked down into the shadowy depths and breathed again. This time too he'd done it. He hadn't fallen. Exhilarated, he ran back all the way to the village.

It was the same every day.

"People in this village shouldn't speak to that boy any more," Crazy Haydar stated, his withered cheeks sunk into the cavities of his toothless mouth. "He's got a curse on him. Every night he goes up there, every night, and . . . I've seen him with my own eyes."

"That's right," Stoneheart Remzi said. He was a former bandit who'd taken to the hills after hacking his sister to pieces. "We must take no notice of him at all. He'll go mad that one, or else he'll yet . . . Who knows . . ."

"Well, I for one will talk to him," Old Meryem declared. Her voice was no louder than the whine of a mosquito. "I wouldn't want the poor boy to die or go mad. It's bad enough for him with his father a ghost."

"Besides, he's such a sweet boy," Zala said. They called her Flirty Zala in the village. "Why, if he were just a little older I'd make him run away with me, I would!"

"I've seen him too, walking on the edge of that precipice," Mustan said, twiddling the hairs of his long sparse beard. "And let me tell you this, it's his father who takes him up there every night, holds him by the hand and makes him walk right on the edge of the precipice. In the dark too! But he'll cast Hassan down the crags one of these days, mark my words . . ."

For some time now his grandmother had refused to talk to him. When he visited her she turned in her bed, her face to the wall, and only moved again, muttering curses under her breath, as he was leaving the room.

This morning he dressed carefully and after making a good breakfast he went straight up to her room.

"Speak to me, Granny. Talk to me about my father. Tell me why he's become a ghost. Tell me how he's to be saved. Speak. Is it true that he's being devoured by worms and vermin? Tell me . . ."

That's what they said. They were eating him up, Halil, the worms, every day, and then every night he rose from his grave, a ghost . . .

"How is it that he's eaten up like that, Granny?"

But she obstinately refused to say a word to him.

It was the same with his uncles, his cousins, the village children . . . Sometimes it seemed to him that even his mother was dumb.

The sun was beating down on Hassan's head and the stream alongside flowed in an incandescent glow.

He was running away, pressing on down Dumlu way, to where Dumlu Castle trembled in a reddish veil of smoke. The hot dust burnt his bare feet and he was dying of thirst.

The cool southwester began to blow as evening fell and still Hassan did not take a pause, not even to refresh himself at the stream and quench his thirst. But now his legs were dragging him backwards. He was afraid of what lay before him, afraid of what he had left behind.

Suddenly, he wheeled about and without knowing it found himself speeding back to the village. It was midnight when he reached the foot of the Anavarza crags. They loomed above him, soaring higher in the darkness. Booming sounds came from up the old ramparts and also the howl of a large animal in pain. The wind shook the trees and bushes and rocks.

As fast as he could Hassan clambered up and came panting to the foot of the ramparts. His hands and feet were cut and bleeding, but he did not hesitate. He went at once to the edge of the precipice and started balancing himself on the knife-edged rocks, walking as on a tightrope. There was a thundering roar in his ears. The thought of the yawning depths below made him sway, but he kept on, taut, quivering, drunk with terror.

Suddenly, a shadowy figure rose in front of him. Hassan cast himself down to the side. In the same instant the figure was on him, pressing upon his chest. He screamed, but not a sound came out of him. Then, gradually the stranglehold on his throat relaxed and he began to breathe again.

After a while he rose. His knees were shaking, but once more he climbed onto the razor edge of the precipice and started balancing himself, walking from one end to the other, ever more recklessly, just as though he were performing a light country dance.

The dawn found him still tottering along the rock edge. Far down below, all whirling together in one dizzy mass, he saw the stream, only a tiny rivulet now, narrow ribbons that were the roads, ant-like people. A finger-sized red truck swirled in the dust. Round and round it went as Hassan collapsed into a cleft among the rocks.

For a long time he did not move. The sun was high now, the rocks hot. Hassan was sweating, but he lay there in a daze, not even knowing whether it was day or night. Translucent red snakes glided between the rocks, casting a ruddy glow about them. His father Halil, swathed in his white shroud, was killing them. At every blow sparks shot up into the sky and fell back in a shower of stars. Yet the snakes reared up again and again before they dropped dead. Hard-cased lustrous insects rattled across the rocks and paths. Small button-sized white snails were plastered over the bushes, the trees, the flowers, over every blade of grass, millions and millions ...

He tried to raise his limp body, but the pain was too much for him. Yet he must get up, he must, in spite of his fears, his dizziness, he must walk once more on the sharp narrow edge of the precipice. He felt he would die if he didn't. Dragging himself to the rocks, he heaved himself up and gazed out at the remote depths. The vast plain stretched on, perfectly flat, right up to the foothills of the Gavur Mountains. Hemité Castle, Yilankalé, Toprakkalé* were wrapped in a haze, but the plain was aglow, bathed in light. Only the chasm below loured darkly, threatening. Hassan did not look down. Rallying his last remaining strength, he leaped onto the rocks and moved forward, walking with one foot almost treading the emptiness. It was worse, much more terrifying in the daylight.

* All old medieval castles.

73

His head whirled, his body went limp. He could not take another step. He stood there, on the edge of the void, swaying backward and forward, knowing he could not but fall. His eyes were blacking out, then in turn being blinded by a strong dazzling light. And the deafening roar in his ears increased as he swayed.

At last he sank back senseless onto the rocks. If he had fainted in his forward motion, he would now have been lying smashed to pieces on the marble-paved surface below. The eagles, swarming in hundreds, would have picked at his flesh and finished him even as he fell.

The white-shrouded figure had come again, driving a horde of red snakes before him.

"Hassan," he was saying, "aren't you my son Hassan, my very own progeny? Can't you save your father? Here you see me, herding hundreds of red snakes, but they're not really snakes at all. Every one of them is a man whose murder has not been avenged, who is doomed to haunt the world as a red snake, and the demons of hell have made me their shepherd. A shepherd of red serpents, Hassan! How can you bear to see your father in this state, how? Have you no pity? Aaah, to crush the serpent, Hassan, to crush the serpent ..."

Dead swallows, flames, stones from the ramparts hailed down upon Hassan. He took to his heels, running for his life, fleeing before that horde of red serpents ...

The village was humming with talk again. Esmé and the ghost of Halil were on everyone's tongue from seven to seventy. Halil had come back, they said. People had seen him. It was his mother he'd gone to first. And afterwards, longing for his village, he'd come to sit there, under a fragrant orange tree. People swore they'd heard his voice crying out in anguish.

"A shepherd of snakes, they've made me, the demons of hell, of red flaming snakes. And then they'll turn me into a long transparent red serpent ... Ah good people, please don't let me be a serpent! If only they would crush the serpent ... Ah, to crush the serpent ..."

Then, with a great bang, he had burst into fragments and red snakes had started to rain over the village.

The grandmother seemed to have relented. There was a soft look on her face as she greeted Hassan. She made him sit down and stroked his hair for a while. She even spoke to him. Hassan was overjoyed. That meant people would start talking to him again. This time too, he had been spared. He drank in her words with rapt attention.

"Halil rises from his grave because of his black passion, my Hassan. Did you know that? It's jealousy makes him haunt the village. How can I lie here, he says, how can I rest if she gives herself to another man, my own peerless beauty? Ah, my Hassan, that your father's bed should be so defiled! Your brave handsome father ... Come, come nearer to me, my child. Listen!"

She drew him to her breast and went on in a whisper.

"How can you know, my darling, you're still a child, though you've grown into a sturdy lad these last years, almost a man ... How can a mother with a stalwart son like you do such things? How can she take a man into her bed every night? It's a fact and not a person in this village who doesn't know it. Even then, even though your father's blood lies unavenged, no one can bring himself to kill her. Because she's so beautiful. And no one ever will. But you, my Hassan, what's to become of you? How will you ever be able to look people in the face? Won't you be disgraced for ever? All your life people will speak of you as Hassan, the son of that whore.

Never, never till kingdom come will you efface that stigma. I've not long to live, Hassan. And what shall I leave behind me? A son killed and unavenged, a grandson with a blot on his name . . ."

She held his head away from her and looked at him. His face was deathly pale. She had struck home at last. Children could be jealous even of a mother, a father . . .

"It's no use waiting up nights to try and surprise her," she went on, elated. "Your mother's very cunning. A woman who's bent on deceiving her husband will always find a way. She can get together with her lover, making her husband hold her drawers for her, and he not a whit the wiser. So don't expect to see anything for yourself. Go out into the village and see if there's anyone left who doesn't know about your mother's goings-on with other men."

On and on she talked, always stressing Esmé's fatal, irresistible beauty.

Hassan left her side reeling, an unbearable ache in his heart. He could not help himself. He made straight for the village square and found that whoever he met was now willing, even eager to talk to him.

And so he listened. For a month, for two months he listened to people telling tales about his mother's whoring. Their words haunted his mind. He was forever seeing a beautiful woman's legs, her face, her body, naked, enfolded in some man's embrace. It was driving him mad, yet still he listened. He must hear what they were saying, he had to know.

As for the villagers, it was as though the grandmother had cast a charm over them all. Whatever she said they repeated over and over again, enlarging upon it a hundredfold. The grandmother held the whole village under a sinister spell, even Hassan. His mother would die. Esmé must die . . .

*

76

"This is too much, brother. Too much for a man to bear."

"If this doesn't kill Hassan, if he can stomach his mother's whoring ..."

"Then there's no blood in him!"

"Well, if there was, would he have suffered his father's murderer to live on another minute, even though it be his mother?"

"He's got tainted blood, tainted ..."

"They say that when a man comes at night to his mother, strips her naked and begins to do his stuff, Hassan stands by and watches. And gets a kick out of it too!"

"Gaping ... All eyes!"

"Even his mother felt some shame once. Go away, she said, does a man ever look at his mother like this? And what do you know? Hassan burst into tears. But I want to, he bawled. I want to see it all."

"Imagine! He enjoys seeing his mother billing and cooing with any fellow that comes along!"

"He even threatened to kill her."

"If you take a man into your bed when I'm not there to see, he said, if you dare to keep it secret from me ..."

"Now what did his mother say to that?"

"What could the poor wretch say? I'm a widow, she said. They've killed my husband, so I need a man. It's a shameful thing for a son to look on while his mother's making love, but if I can't stop you, what can I do? I can't live without men."

"That she can't!"

"She's like an Arab mare in heat, that one."

"She'd handle all the men of the village in a single night."

"Yes, and cry out for more in broad daylight!"

"But what can Hassan do about all this? He's only a child."

"Nonsense, he's a grown lad, damn him!"

"How can he just stand by and look on his mother's private parts and all?"

"But how can the boy know? If his own mother takes a man into her bed, how can he know it's wrong?"

"If you ask me, I think he's just biding his time."

"Heh! What patience!"

"Well, that's how it is. Would any child, especially a child like Hassan, bear to see his mother whoring and not do something about it?"

"A man can bear anything except to have a whore for a mother."

"Just you wait! One of these days ..."

"He's a crack shot Hassan, you know. He'll finish her off, and the man covering her too."

"Don't make me laugh! Doesn't Esmé know this? Why doesn't she take the precaution to hide herself from Hassan? Because she's sure as death he'll never touch a hair of her head."

"That't true enough. She's his mother after all and the most beautiful woman in the world. Such a beautiful woman has to be generous with herself ..."

"How can Halil forget such a beauty? He comes to her in the guise of a red snake. A huge snake, that long, but transparent, a red snake you can see through ..."

"Poor Halil, he coils himself up in front of her, just to gaze at his Esmé. And then he sees her with all those other men. A ghost, a poor ghost ... There's nothing he can do about it."

"Only a snake, transparent, made of thin air! How can he take his revenge?"

"But there's still Hassan to be reckoned with. You people don't really know Hassan. He's not one to bear with a whoring mother."

"But he's only a child! And anyway, how could anyone kill Esmé?"

"A beauty the like of which Allah will never make again . . ."

"And these people want to kill her, just because that doddering old crone tells them to!"

"Enemies of beauty, they are, enemies of Allah!"

"Allah who so proudly fashioned her . . ."

"Well, it would've been better if he hadn't. She's just a curse on us all."

"But why? Why? There's no harm in her."

"No harm! Who is it, then, strolls through the village day in day out, swinging her hips and turning every man's head?"

"It's such a pity for her . . ."

"Then let her go back to her village."

"She won't."

"She wouldn't! They say there are a hundred beauties like her in that village. Here, she's the only one . . ."

"Don't talk nonsense. As if Allah had the time to make another Esmé, let alone a hundred! She's unique."

"There isn't another woman to match her."

"And to think she's going to be killed!"

"By her own son too!"

"Ah, the godless son! To kill his own mother . . ."

"They'd do anything in that family."

"Ready to kill they are, every man of them. They'd wipe out not only a mother, but their whole race if they had the chance."

"Poor Esmé."

"They'll have her killed."

"Hassan will do it."

"And he being a child they can't send him to prison either."

"They'll all get off scot-free . . ."

*

79

And then, one day, all the talk and gossip was cut short and an unnatural stillness fell over the village. It seemed to Hassan that no one spoke anymore, not a single villager, not a word, not a murmur. Every day he paid a visit to his grandmother, but she too never opened her mouth either. She might just as well have been dead, and all the others too. Was it because they had stopped talking about his father and mother? The subject was forgotten, buried away as though it had never existed. Hassan wandered about the village, looking hopefully, almost pleadingly, at whoever he came across, but ... Nothing ... He could have talked to the trees and streams and begged for mercy, he could have done anything to break this awful silence.

The swallows were no more, their twittering hushed, their nests empty. Eagles still swirled in the depths of the skies, but not a swish of their wings could be heard. All those red snakes and insects, the phantoms in their long white shrouds, the yellow dogs that bayed every night in the graveyard, everything had vanished without a trace. The world was utterly empty.

As a last hope he went to the precipice below the ramparts of Anavarza Castle and began to walk along the razor-like crags on its edge. The sun beat down mercilessly upon him. One slip and he would hurtle down the craggy depths, dashed to pieces. To pieces! He tried to figure to himself the horror of it, yet he felt nothing, no fear, not the slightest tremor. Down below, the trucks still crept along the roads like toy things, people were only ants and the wide stream a narrow ribbon on the plain. But his head was perfectly steady and it seemed that even if he fell he would never know fear again.

His eyes fixed on the yawning depths, he attempted to summon some emotion, some feeling akin to fear, but in vain. He broke into a run, dashing along that razor's edge, wheeling, running again. Nothing happened, nothing, nothing . . .

He gave it up and rushed back home. His mother was there, and all at once a racking shudder shook him from top to toe. Quivering with dread, he escaped into the village. But even as he ran that unbearable void enveloped him again. He must go back . . .

Near his mother, he was seized with terror, trembling of all his limbs, beside himself. Far from her he was bereft of life, utterly drained.

Esmé had fired the earth-oven in the yard and flames were leaping up from the hole.

Hassan stood at a distance, playing with a revolver. It was his father's revolver. As the flames subsided, his mother bent over the oven. Hassan was shaking again. His flesh crept and his head whirled. Only his mother stood out clearly in front of his eyes. She was surrounded by flames. Suddenly, the revolver he was holding exploded. There was a piercing scream. The revolver burst out again, and again.

An odour of burning hair and flesh mounted in the air. Everything went blank for Hassan. The revolver dangling from his hand, he stagggered round and round the oven in which his mother's head was buried, her hair aflame. Then he turned and fled towards the Anavarza crags.

Three days later his dog tracked him down in that ancient Roman sarcophagus. The lid was drawn almost shut over him. The dog must have followed his smell right up into the crags, his master's smell.

A few months ago, I saw Hassan again. He came to visit me where I am living now and told me how well he was faring.

He owned plenty of land, three harvesters, five tractors ... He had built a mansion for himself, set in seven acres of orange groves, and he couldn't have enough of describing its splendour to me. He had got married too. A lovely wife he had, and six children by now, three boys and three girls.

We reminisced on our prison days, on that Agha who had killed four people, but still performed his *namaz* prayers five times a day, on the cowardly wretch Lütfi ... Hassan said that back in the Chukurova people were becoming worse and worse, cruel, hard, inhuman. There was not a man you could call a friend anymore. Ready to gouge each other's eyes out they were, for a mere five *kurush* a man would kill his own father ... Hassan himself avoided mixing among them as much as he could. His home was so beautiful, the orange flowers smelled so good in the spring ...

Also by Yashar Kemal

MEMED, MY HAWK

Ince Memed, only son of a poor widow, is brought up in servitude to the Agha, or lord, of five villages in the Taurus highlands of Anatolia. His plans to escape with his beloved, Hatché, are dashed when the Agha overtakes the fleeing couple. Memed puts up a fierce resistance, wounds the Agha and escapes in the darkness, but Hatché is captured. Memed, still only a youth, becomes a brigand in the mountains; his two ambitions are to rescue his beloved and to settle accounts with the powerful, vindictive Agha.

"A tale that assumes epic proportions and gathers speed to rush to a spectacular climax"   *Daily Telegraph*

"A beautiful novel in the old, glorious tradition of heroic storytelling"   *Scotsman*

"Follows in that tradition of strong, simple novels about the life of the peasantry. It has that insider's feelings for man, the oppressed, labouring animal ... you might find in Tolstoy, Hardy or Silone. The author never loses his freshness, an ability to pick on details as though seen for the first time"
Guardian

Also by Yashar Kemal

THE WIND FROM THE PLAIN

Each year the wind brings the news to old Halil's keen senses that the cotton is ripe for picking in the plain, and at his word the entire population of his remote village in the Taurus Mountains set out on the arduous trek to earn by their toil enough to pay their debts and buy the necessities of life for the bitter highland winter.

But this year old Halil finds himself too old to go on foot; so does Long Ali's ageing mother Meryemdje, and both clamour for a place on the back of Long Ali's broken-down nag, once a pure-bred Arab steed stolen by Ali's brigand father, now scarcely capable of bearing either of the two old people. Halil's determination to stay on and Meryemdje's to get him off lead to a war of words and cunning which lights with delicious comedy the sombre drama of the march. But when the decrepit animal finally dies, and the group falls behind the rest of the villagers, it is the unfortunate Ali who has to show piety towards his mother and compassion to old Halil, while pressing on with dogged resolution to reach the cotton fields before they are picked bare.

The power of *The Wind from the Plain*, the first volume of *The Wind from the Plain* trilogy, lies in its simplicity, which in turn lies in the handful of down-to-earth characters whose story it tells – the timeless one of survival.

"... has the freshness and vigour of a writer who, one suspects, is the exultant discoverer of virgin territory ... it asserts its stature as literature"   *Spectator*

Also by Yashar Kemal

IRON EARTH, COPPER SKY

After a bad season the poor mountain villagers, who pick cotton for their livelihood, are unable to pay their creditor, the shop-keeper Adil Effendi. Such a break with age-old tradition causes them to be overwhelmed with a sense of guilt. They wait in terror for Adil to come, but he fails to appear and in his inexplicable absence his figure swells till it fills their minds and they become sick with the apprehension of some terrible disaster. In their despair they look to Tashbash, a brave man, one of themselves, who has always stood up for them against the tyranny of Sefer, their Headman.

They invest Tashbash with all the virtues, and to these miraculous power is gradually added. What this does to Tashbash, his innocent doubts and mental torment, the fate that comes upon him and the very apposite conclusion combine to make a moving story alive with acute observation of human nature, containing passages of lyrical beauty and deep compassion.

Iron Earth, Copper Sky is the second volume of *The Wind from the Plain* trilogy, a sequel to *The Wind from the Plain*.

"Yashar Kemal is one of the modern world's great story-tellers"   JOHN BERGER

"This strange and lyrical book, beautifully translated by Thilda Kemal, has the compulsive power of a tale told to a wondering audience beside a flickering fire"

Daily Telegraph

Also by Yashar Kemal

THE UNDYING GRASS

Memidik, the young hunter, is obsessed by the urge to kill the tyrannous headman, Sefer, who has caused him much pain and humiliation. But each time he tries, the figure of Sefer looms many times larger than life, and Memidik freezes in fear. But his accidental slaying of another man fires him with renewed determination. Sefer, meanwhile, has been sentenced to solitude as the villagers refuse to speak to him. Sefer's taunting only strengthens their loyalty to their champion Tashbash whom they come to invest with mythical powers. The web of their fantasy becomes so extensive that when he returns to the village, a worn-out man, they cannot recognise or accept him.

The Undying Grass, the third volume in *The Wind from the Plain* trilogy and a sequel to *Iron Earth, Copper Sky*, also continues the story of Ali and his mother Meryemdje who, in their different ways, learn the difficult art of survival.

"Yashar Kemal is a cauldron where fact, fantasy and folklore are stirred to produce poetry. He is a storyteller in the oldest tradition, that of Homer, spokesman for a people who had no other voice"   ELIA KAZAN

"He speaks for those people for whom no one else is speaking"
                                                    JAMES BALDWIN